Storm Dog

Storm Dog

L. M. Elliott

KATHERINE TEGEN BOOKS
An Imprint of HarperCollins Publishers

Also by L. M. Elliott

Da Vinci's Tiger
Give Me Liberty
Hamilton and Peggy!: A Revolutionary Friendship
Annie, Between the States
Under a War-Torn Sky
Across a War-Tossed Sea
A Troubled Peace
Suspect Red
Flying South

Katherine Tegen Books is an imprint of HarperCollins Publishers.

Storm Dog
Copyright © 2020 by Laura Malone Elliott
All rights reserved. Printed in the United States of America.
No part of this book may be used or reproduced in any manner whatsoever without written permission except in the case of brief quotations embodied in critical articles and reviews. For information address HarperCollins Children's Books, a division of HarperCollins Publishers, 195 Broadway, New York, NY 10007.
www.harpercollinschildrens.com

Library of Congress Control Number: 2019956224
ISBN 978-0-06-243000-7

Typography by David DeWitt
20 21 22 23 24   PC/LSCH   10 9 8 7 6 5 4 3 2 1
❖

First Edition

To all the dogs my family has rescued over the years
only to find that they actually saved us.

As ever, to Megan and Peter,
who have a magical way with all manner of creatures
in need of understanding.

And with the most heartfelt thanks
to my favorite teacher, Dr. Ed Wilson,
who taught me to have faith in the sublime in this world.

What would the world be like without music or rivers or the green and tender grass? What would this world be like without dogs?

—Mary Oliver

Prelude

I WAS BORN IN TEMPEST SEASON—in the month of March, when the world has trouble deciding what season it wants to be. Round here in Virginia that means temperatures can swing thirty degrees in a single day. We duck and cover through freak hail storms and wild downpours that explode into being all of a sudden when a hopeful spring breeze stumbles up against leftover winter air that's curled up comfortable and happy against the Blue Ridge Mountains. I swear it makes the cold air mad. *BAM*—there's pushback lightning and thunder, swirling clouds and gales that blow your hair every which way, like the ears of a dog hanging out the window of a car racing along Route 50.

Snowflakes can mingle in tiny cyclones with pink blossoms that winds tear off the branches of flailing fruit trees. Creeks rage into tidal waves of brown terrified water that can knock down high banks of spring bluebells that had just started to rejoice into life. The world is all cacophony, aggravation, and I-can't-figure-out-what-I'm-thinking tantrums.

Sort of the way I feel all the time.

According to my family, I've always been like that, coming into the world during one of those March weather-ragers—thrashing and crying, a seismic surge of sound and sass and questions. Mama calls me the storm child, and she doesn't mean it in a nice way. Maybe that's why she doesn't like me. Too much noise. Too much angst. Just . . . too much. I suppose I get her point. I can't remember a time that winds and waves weren't churning me up inside. But I just don't see the point in being all calm and cool about things. Seems like a whole lot of boring, still pond water to me, no matter how beautiful those glassy reflections are.

That's the way my sister is: smooth, polished to an appealing sheen of perfect pretty. Nothing disquieting or annoying about her. In public anyway.

Everyone says to me, "Why can't you be more like Gloria? Gloria would never break the window." (That was a total accident, by the way. I'd just heard about David and Goliath in Sunday school and was testing out whether a slingshot and stone could really take down a giant. I wasn't aiming for Gloria's window, I swear.) "Gloria would never kick a hole in a door." (My arms were full of books. And nobody would open that stupid door for me!) "Gloria would never walk around with ketchup stains on her shorts." (Honestly, when I eat with my family, things just seem to jump out of my hands.) "Gloria would never pout about a lovely pink ribbon being put in her hair." (It was the size of a baseball mitt, okay?)

Gloria won the Miss Apple Blossom Outstanding Teen contest when she was fifteen. During high school, she starred in all the plays that featured a blond Barbie-doll type character. People started talking about how she was sure to be discovered one day—like Marilyn Monroe was when a photographer just happened to walk into the munitions factory where she was working the assembly line and spotted her. "Child, you are the spitting image of her," the church ladies would coo at Gloria on Sundays.

Now Gloria's nineteen years old, and there's a chance she'll be chosen as one of the Shenandoah Festival princesses for this year's parade. If that happens Gloria will be *really* famous around here, just from sitting and smiling, waving that cupped-hand homecoming-queen salute and floating down Washington Street on a cart decorated with sheets of plastic flowers. I can hear all the church ladies: "When those Hollywood scouts see her in the parade, they'll snap Gloria up. She's going places, for sure." Then they'll probably turn to me and say the type of thing they tossed at me when I snitched cookies from the rectory hall before the service, knocking over pitchers of apple juice onto the church's tablecloths in the process: "Try to be a little like your sister, Ariel. If you don't settle down, the Rapture might pass you over and leave you in H-E-double hockey sticks." (That's HELL, in case you don't speak church lady.)

Yep, that's me—the storm child. Sometimes I worry they might be right. When squalls roar up, spilling zigzag, blue-black shadows across our pastures, ripping up trees and toppling them onto power lines to make sparks fly, it does seem like the devil is trying to take over God's good work. And I kinda like listening to the winds and watching lightning crackle across the horizon like gigantic electrified snakes.

But here's the honest truth—I like the afterward just as much. I love that miracle when a peephole of sunlight breaks through all those angry clouds and then spreads slowly, dissolving the dark into a luminous, heavenly blue. You can smell the earth greening up. And the singing of birds when they've ventured out from their hunkered-down hiding spots, singing in joy at being saved from annihilation—well, they sound like a chorus of angels to me.

I wish people could see that I'd really rather not go to Hell, because when everyone expects you to become a screwup, it's hard to avoid becoming one. Almost like I'd disappoint them if I turned out well.

I suspect that's what led me to my trouble. Although I have to admit the idea did just come to me. Nobody *told* me to do it.

It all began after one of those wild, cymbal-crashing March thunderstorms that took out a bunch of trees just for fun during the night. That and a phone call during breakfast.

One

MY APPLE STRUDEL POP-TART HAD JUST jumped out of the toaster when Gloria's phone danced with Taylor Swift's "Shake It Off." I used to love that feisty musical life-advice until I heard the song a thousand times a week from my sister's pink glitter cell phone. She hadn't seemed to notice that I recently made my ringtone the refrain from another Taylor song: *"Why you gotta be so mean?"*

Gloria answered. "Yes, ma'am, this is me." She mouthed silently at Mama: *It's them.* Mama eased out of her chair and crept toward Gloria to hold her hand. I swear she stopped breathing. Ever heard the term *helicopter mom?* Well, with Gloria, Mama is like an entire air force fighter squadron.

Chewing on her lower lip, Gloria listened for a long minute. Then she smiled and nodded at Mama.

Mama went berserk. She started jumping up and down, tears spurting out of her eyes, and flapping Gloria's arm up and down. Gloria managed to thank the person who'd called and hang up before she started bouncing, too. Around the kitchen they hippity-hopped, squealing—no thuds, no lurching, that perfect spinning-top gyration that only ballerinas and pretty girls can pull off.

And they are pretty, those two. Traffic-stopping beautiful. They both have turquoise-blue eyes, pronounced apple-round high cheekbones, and honey-colored hair that curls gently to frame their faces. They even stand at the same height, petite and slender, just the right size to tuck up under a man's arm. Like twins born twenty-five years apart, I swear.

My hair, on the other hand, is frizzled and mud-colored, my eyes murky hazel, my nose long, my face thin and ending in a chin that juts out like I'm looking for a fight. I am gawky and gangly, a head taller than all my eighth-grade classmates, no matter how much I slouch to hide it. I figure the night I was born the lightning scared the bejeebees out of my mother and the family beauty out of me.

"What's going on?" I asked.

They stopped and looked at me like I was an idiot.

They do that a lot. I have to admit the insult of their acting like I'm dumb as a slug has lately been turning me a little snarky with them in return.

"For pity's sake, Ariel. Gloria's been worried sick waiting for this phone call."

"Why? Who was it?" I paused. "Was it . . . was it Hollywood?" I whispered, parroting the church ladies. I know, being sarcastic like that isn't nice.

"No. The committee," they answered in unison. They do that a lot, too—speaking the same words at the same time.

"What committee?"

"The Apple Blossom Festival Committee." This was said slowly with dramatic emphasis on each word. I'm surprised they didn't add "duuuuh" at the end.

With that, Mama was done with me.

Of course, she'd been done with me for a long time, really. Ever since it'd become pretty obvious that my ugly-duckling phase may be a permanent thing. I think my existence embarrasses Mama. Like if that legendary artist Michelangelo had once flubbed a piece of sculpture so badly that each time he produced something Gloria-gorgeous—like his famous seventeen-foot-tall *David*—people still pointed at the boo-boo statue and undercut his best achievement with saying, "Well, yes, but don't forget about that hunk of junk over there. . . ." Which would be me for Mama.

Mama turned to my father. "Ed!" She half gasped in her excitement.

Daddy remained lost in the *Washington Post* op-ed page. He still reads a print newspaper front to back, every day.

"Edward!" She tried stern.

Nothing.

Mama went for her tried-and-true, singsongy whine, "Ed-dieee."

Daddy looked up from his newspaper. "Yes, sweetheart?"

Mama sighed. She pulled the paper out of his hands and plopped down on his lap. Now, a forty-five-year-old woman sitting on a guy like he's a Santa Claus seems pretty infantile and weird to me. It also wrinkles the heck out of Daddy's crisply ironed khakis. But Daddy blinked behind his horn-rimmed glasses to refocus and smiled up at Mama—that dreamy grin he always gets when gazing at her.

"Gloria has been picked to be one of the Apple Blossom Festival princesses. She'll be riding on the main float in the parade."

"Ah, just like you, sweetheart."

"Yes! Just like me!" She kissed him on his nose and straightened his bow tie.

He said something gooey and kissed her back before she jumped up and started dancing again with Gloria.

For a second, I thought I might upchuck my Pop-Tart. Their PDA just gets to me sometimes. I wondered fleetingly if I could aim well enough to spew Mama with vomit. Then I looked over at Daddy, hoping he'd say a little something nice to me like, "That'll be you, Ariel, in a few years." As if. He just went back to his coffee and headlines, engulfed in his morning fog of thought and news.

I'd already given up on Mama. And on Gloria. But Daddy? I keep thinking there's hope for Daddy and me. Ever since my brother, George, left for Afghanistan, my having a decent relationship with Daddy has felt even more important.

I should probably tell you a few things about my daddy. He's a public defender, the lawyer who stands up in court and argues the rights of people who've been accused of crimes and don't have enough money to hire a lawyer. So the state gives them one—like my daddy. Yeah, I know a parent being a cop or a prosecutor— the people who make sure the bad guys are caught and go to jail—is easier for a daughter to brag on. But I'm proud of him just the same because Daddy's an "ideals" man. Even when he's defending some tool who robbed a 7-Eleven, Daddy's standing on principle, safeguarding our constitutional rights.

What makes our country great, according to Daddy, is the fact that all of us—rich or poor—have "inalienable" rights. Every life matters the same in the U.S. of A., he says. That means all of us have the right to be heard in court without prejudice: presumed innocent until proven guilty beyond any reasonable doubt—and without any shenanigans going on during an arrest. There's due process, rules of law that must be followed. That protects us from things like racial profiling—police stopping and arresting someone because they assume a guy's trouble just because he's a person of color or an immigrant—and from people in power deciding they don't like us or our opinions and making up ways to lock us up and shut us up.

Mama had paused now in her hippity-hoppity celebration gyration to let Gloria text her bazillion friends. "I'm in!" Gloria said aloud as her thumbs speed-tapped her message over and over.

With each responding chime she squealed.

Mama too. "What about Liza Lee's daughter?" she whispered.

Gloria texted. A long, long, loooooonnnng pause. Gloria made an OMG face that could launch a thousand memes. *NO*, she mouthed. Then she texted furiously, answers ping-ponging back.

Mama smirked. "Serves that conceited cow right. Hear that, Eddie? That stuck-up snob whose family has been pushing people around forever just because her ancestors have been here since the Revolution— her daughter is *not* a princess." Noticing Daddy wasn't paying attention, Mama broke off her gloating attack on Liza Lee, putting her hands on her hips. "Eddie."

Daddy turned the page of his newspaper and read on.

You've probably figured out that my daddy is in his own head a lot. (He was a philosophy major at the University of Virginia—that should tell you everything!) As a teenager, he was also a serious protester during the tail end of the Vietnam War. If you're good at math and know some history, you're also probably calculating right now that Daddy is kind of old. You're right—he's in his sixties! (But don't worry, he jogs and eats kale chips like a fiend.)

Mama is his second wife.

At our annual Christmas parade of horses and riders, I've heard plenty of pearl-clad women whisper that Daddy is still "a handsome devil." The next thing they whisper is, "Such a pity." It took me a long time to discover what the "pity" was that they were referring to. It's my mama. Now, Mama and I have never gotten along. We have nothing in common—I mean, I love books and she loves *Real Housewives of Beverly Hills*. But I still think the gossip about her and Daddy is mean.

For one thing, calling her "white trash" is pretty darn antiquated and snotty. But by tradition and topography, this area has a split personality, with the Blue Ridge being the spine dividing the ribs. In a lot of ways, we're like March weather: stark hot-and-cold differences bump up against each other all the time, making for some pretty outrageous friction and name-calling. We're talking serious self-identity crisis stuff.

East of the mountains, huge old-Virginia horse estates still carpet most of Fauquier and parts of Loudoun counties, green and lush and genteel. Long-time residents speak in commonwealth drawls, attend historic fieldstone Episcopal churches, and know how to post a horse's trot. Daddy comes from that elite, country-gentry stratosphere.

Just over the mountains past the Shenandoah River,

the land turns rocky as it rolls toward the West Virginia border. Fields spit out boulders like the wads of chewing tobacco some people there *kersplat.* That's Mama's territory. Here and there in the crooks of the hills are shanties and trailer parks. Voices turn twangy. Churches might sport lit-up neon crosses and signs with catchy warnings like: *Know God, be saved. No God, be damned.*

Hayfields and horse pastures give way to an ocean of corn and the real glory of the place, apple orchards. Of course, you get your hands dirty picking apples in a way you don't when asking your stable-manager to saddle up your thoroughbred for the hunt.

I live toward the east, in a big ole brick house with fireplaces in every room that my daddy's great-great-grandfather built in 1800-something. But I am definitely a mixed breed. To me there's nothing as beautiful as the low mountains to the west, frosted pink in the spring with apple tree blossoms and the constant winds rattling them.

Those famous cherry blossoms along the Tidal Basin in Washington, DC—they don't even come close. I've seen them. They're only an hour's drive from here. Do they even grow cherries people can eat? Sure, they symbolize diplomacy and international peace since Japan gave them to us. But here's the difference: ever bitten into an apple that you've picked straight off a branch? Crunch into peel that's still slightly warm from the sun and had that sweet juice baptize your face? It'll change your life.

That's what the Shenandoah Apple Blossom Festival and parade have been celebrating since 1924. The blooming of the orchards, the promise of apples to come, the gifts of this earth, the joy of life. And that's where Daddy laid eyes on Mama for the first time. I suspect that's why the Festival is so all-fire important to Mama.

Daddy's first wife—George's mother, a "women's lib" lawyer—had died from cancer. George was only two years old at the time. Daddy, devastated, was seen carrying him everywhere, like a teddy bear, almost. Even into court.

Then came Mama. She floated down Winchester's streets in her billowing pink dress, an exquisite, vibrant, twenty-one-year-old Festival princess. I think maybe, after all the sadness of his wife's sickness, someone so pretty and fresh and full of life was as irresistible to him as a Shenandoah apple to a starving man. Six months later, Daddy married Mama. His mother keeled over dead the very next day.

A few years after, Mama produced Gloria. George was five years old. I arrived four years after that, when

Daddy was already fifty. He calls me their *"quelle belle surprise."* (Mama always snorts at that and says, "Yes, Ariel's a surprise, that's for sure.")

Frankly, my parents are so different, they never have much to talk about. But it didn't seem to worry them any. Mostly Daddy talked to my brother George and once in a while to me when he noticed I was reading a book he had liked as a child or listening to some of his rock 'n' roll vinyl albums. That satisfied me fine. But Daddy hasn't done a whole lot of looking at anything except those newspapers since George went off to fight in Afghanistan.

Mama snapped her fingers at Daddy's fancy virtual voice assistant and commanded, "Play Van Morrison's 'Gloria.'"

As the sounds of a 1960s electric guitar, keyboard organ, and backbeat drums blasted through the kitchen, Mama pulled Daddy to his feet and knocked his newspaper to the floor. Following Van Morrison's gravelly voice, Mama shouted what seemed to be her personal anthem, lyrics I'd heard way too many times about her baby, the daughter who made her feel "all right:"

"...her name is G...L...O...R...I-i-i-i-i...
G-L-O-R-I-A,
Gloooooooo—ria..."

When Mama pulled Gloria into a triangle with Daddy to dance, I got up and headed for the hills. I don't think the three of them even heard the back-porch door slam behind me—even though I whammed it hard three times to give them the chance.

Two

THAT SPECTACLE WOULD NOT HAVE HAPPENED if George were home. He would've winked at me with a yeah-I-know-they-are-ridiculous expression and guided me into the dance, elbowing me into the family circle. But without George I have no wingman.

I pulled my bike out from the old hay barn that serves as our garage. Throwing myself on it, I pedaled hard down the gravel backcountry lanes that run along our pastures. Puddles left over from the previous night's thunder-gusher splashed and soaked me with mud. But I didn't stop. I felt possessed with the kind of fury that comes from being left out in the cold.

I veered onto the open paved curves. These roads are hazardous enough for cars and near suicidal for bikers. But that danger never stops the Sunday cyclists from whipping through here in their tight, neon outfits. It wasn't going to stop me either.

I was heading for Sky Meadows State Park. George and I used to go there to lose our troubles and touch the clouds and climb to the mystical Appalachian trails that American Indians forged with moccasin-clad feet once upon a long time ago. The ancient track is sheltered by a forest of maples, pin oaks, hickories, and dogwood trees. You should see the colors in the fall—fiery reds, oranges, and golds mixed together helter-skelter, wherever birds dropped their seeds or an acorn rolled.

People come from all over to drive in gawking traffic jams along the Skyline Drive to experience nature's extraordinary color wheel. The real delight, though, is to get out and walk the Blue Ridge's shaded pathways. Every so often they take the hiker to the edge of a crag for a mind-blowing view of the emerald valleys below. It must be amazing to be a hawk and get that kind of cloud-down perspective on the world all the time.

Winded, I *eeeked* slowly up the ascending park road, swaying my bike back and forth with each pedal to give myself momentum. I ditched it by Mount Bleak House, the fieldstone home that holds the hilltop. My legs were already wobbly tired from the three-mile ride. But I marched stubbornly up the hillside for twenty minutes to keep from breaking down in baby-tears.

I can't stand crying—it makes my head hurt.

Of course, there seems to be an art to crying that I just don't get. Gloria pouts and sighs, and tears diamond up around her eyes. When a tiny pendant dribbles down her dimpled face, ever so feminine, everyone around her just melts. "Don't cry, sugar." "Oh my, what in the world is wrong?" "Let me fix it for you, sweet cakes."

Me? I cry loud. My eyes turn red. My nose runs. Everyone tells me to stop having a tantrum. They say, "Gracious, what a thunderclap."

So, you can imagine who wins parental sympathy when Gloria and I squabble. Daddy is good about holding court and giving us both our say. That's the lawyer in him, sure. But I swear Gloria just flat out lies or finds a way to pin her actions on others in self-righteous martyrdom. Daddy doesn't see it. He's got the same blind spot for her that he does for Mama. I sure hope Daddy can read his clients and witnesses better than he does those two. Or the justice system is in deep trouble.

Reaching the meadow plateaus of hip-high grass, I lay down to rest in a patch warmed by sunshine. I made myself breathe in, breathe out, in-out, to push away my anger enough to pull in the mystical power of the hillsides. It was the last week of March. The grass from last year was stiff and yellowed, but pushing up through it were ribbons of new life, slender fresh-green blades. It's like that poem by Robert Frost—do you know him? "Nature's first green is gold."

I keep a notebook of quotes that explain better what I am feeling than I can say myself. Bits of songs. Passages from books. Lines of poetry. I also make lists of books I hear of that sound interesting and want to read. Right now I'm knee deep in *To Kill a Mockingbird*. I see a lot of Atticus Finch in my daddy, actually. And a lot of Scout's hometown, Maycomb, in my world—in terms of attitudes and characters and the big division between those who've had opportunities handed them and those who haven't. Of course, Virginia isn't Alabama or Alabama, Virginia. That's a big mistake outsiders always make—Hollywood, for instance—that all the states below Pennsylvania are exactly the same. That would be like saying New Jersey and Maine are identical.

George gave me that notebook right before he deployed. So it is very precious to me. He'd found me in our house's library the week before he left for Afghanistan, the summer after I finished sixth grade, sitting in a pile of books I'd pulled off the shelf because I liked the sounds of their titles. William Faulkner's *The*

Sound and the Fury, for instance. Doesn't that sound like perfect reading for a storm child?

To me, our family library is as exciting as a pyramid and all its treasures must be to the archeologists who unearth them. When it's rainy or cold and I can't escape to the hills from Mama's tirades, I spend whole days curled up in its old deep-cushy armchairs. Its floor-to-ceiling bookcases are stuffed with leather-bound volumes with crisp, thick pages inscribed with worlds begging to be explored. The room smells like what I imagine the club cars in an old-timey transcontinental train did. As transporting to magic as the Polar Express. The perfect place for me to hide from my life and escape to others'.

"Hey, A!" George was leaning against the door. ("A"— that's the cool nickname he gave me. You probably think, sure, Ariel starts with *A*, but George said he started calling me that because I was always getting *A*s at school. Isn't he the best?) "You've got enough books there to build a fort." He'd done that with me plenty when we were younger, using leftover telephone books we found in the attic to stack up in battlements. "Dad's pretty protective of those really old ones, you know. First editions. Don't hurt them."

"I'm not building a fort, George. I'm reading!" I held up *The Old Man and the Sea* by Ernest Hemingway. I have to admit I was struggling a bit to understand it.

George whistled and then made a face when he saw what I'd pulled out. "Kinda adult stuff, A," he said gently.

"So? I can read them!"

"I know you can. You are such a smarty-pants. But maybe . . ." He reached over to one of the shelves and pulled out *The Horse and His Boy* from the Narnia series. "I really loved that one. Try it instead. Or maybe this one." He handed me *Kidnapped* by Robert Louis Stevenson. He glanced around and seemed to get more and more uncomfortable, murmuring, "She needs some stuff from this century if she's ever going to fit in."

I know he didn't mean for me to hear, but I did. It hit me kinda hard that George thought I was a freak, too. But I didn't say anything because he turned around and announced, "I'm going to make a list of some books you might like, A. We can talk about them when we email. Would you like that?"

My head almost popped off, I was nodding so hard.

The very next day George gave me that notebook. This is what he had scribbled in it:

I know these books might seem a little young to you at first, A, given your grown-up tastes, but start with them. I bet some other kids at school will have read them and would like to talk

with you about them: <u>Maniac Magee</u>; <u>My Side of the Mountain</u>;
<u>Bud, Not Buddy</u>; <u>Shiloh</u>; and <u>The Giver</u>. Then move on to <u>The</u>
<u>Perks of Being a Wallflower</u>, <u>A Separate Peace</u>, and <u>Catcher in</u>
<u>the Rye</u>.

Emma (that's George's girlfriend) *says you'll love <u>Ella</u>*
<u>Enchanted</u>, Tamora Pierce's Protector of the Small series,
<u>Stargirl</u>, most anything by Judy Blume, the Divergent trilogy,
and <u>Wicked</u>. She also thinks you'll like a poet named Emily
Dickinson.

Here's my favorite quote. My mantra to life, really. It's from
an American writer named Thoreau. You'll read about him in
high school. He said: "When I hear music, I fear no danger. I
am invulnerable."

Find out what does that for you, A. Okay?

Don't ever forget I love you, kiddo.

Printed on the cover of that notebook is a saying from
a guy named Emerson, a friend of George's Thoreau.
Drink the Wild Air.

Yup. Sucking into my lungs and soul the afterward
air of a rock-the-world-deluge, all rain-washed and
redeemed and slap-yourself-in-the-face fresh—that's one
of the few things that can make me feel "invulnerable."
For a few minutes anyway.

Everyone should be able to find hope in the world

waking up and preening after a storm. Like those teeny peepers that come to life around here as soon as winter's had its last blast—frogs only as big as my little toe, bursting out of thick, snow-melt mud and partying in a song that's a hundred times their size. Their symphony resounds in the air and through the woods and can't help but make a person smile. If you're paying attention.

Just saying.

That's the kind of peace I was searching for that morning. I rolled over onto my belly and rested my face on crossed arms so I could gaze through the grasses. Up on these low mountains the wind never completely dies down, so the world's always shifting a bit. The grasses hum as the breeze ripples them. I closed my eyes and listened.

Three

AS I LAY THERE, SCENES OF George sang to me.

Scene One: I was on our rope swing, hanging long from our front-lawn oak tree. I was six years old, George fifteen.

"Push me higher, George."

"You sure, honey?"

"Higher! Higher!"

George pushed. I soared, my gut lurching. My toes nearly brushed leaves.

"Higher!"

"No way, kiddo. You'll fall off."

"Higher! Higher!" I shouted, kicking my legs.

"No! That's enough." George stepped back, his arms by his sides.

"I'll tell Mama that you were smooching in the barn with Emma."

"What? Okay, I warned you." Annoyed, George shoved. "Hang on!"

But I didn't hang on. As the swing catapulted higher and then dove back to earth, I lost my grip. I felt myself swimming in air.

"Ariel!"

Somehow George got his body between the ground and me. We hit hard. I was fine. George broke his wrist.

He never told Daddy and Mama what a brat I was being or that he had saved me. He claimed he'd been swinging too high and had fallen.

Scene Two: "Ariel, you are such a pain!" Gloria screeched at me. "Take that off."

She and Mama collect American Girl dolls. I wonder if Gloria ever actually played with them. They were lined up in rows, on display, and she had a bazillion outfits for them. I knew better than to pull them off the shelves. But I'd snitched a frilly baby bonnet and stuffed it onto a disreputable stray cat I'd found in the barn. I was trying to beautify it a bit with the hopes of turning it into a house pet.

Gloria was yelling and trying to grab the cat from me when George showed up. "Hold on, girls, hold on." He pulled us apart. We blibber-blabbered our explanations of how the other was being a total jerk. George got this funny look on his face. He undid that baby bonnet from the cat and plopped it on his own head. Shocked, we stopped arguing. When he stuck his thumb in his mouth and "goo-goo-blah-blah-ed," even Gloria laughed. He took off running, and the two of us darted after, giggling and romping.

Scene Three: "Whatcha doing, Georgie?" I was standing in his door, watching him be-bop his head, a blissful smile on his handsome face. He wore big headphones so his room was silent, but he obviously was wreathed in music.

Around his neck hung his saxophone. George was a high school senior and had become a kick-butt musician, making it into All-State Band every year. That's a *big* deal. He was the drum major of the marching band, too. Somehow he made that goofy uniform with all its buttons and spats and ridiculous tall furry hat look cool. But what he loved most was jazz band. When George stood up to play his improv solos, everyone within earshot froze, mesmerized by the sound of his soul crooning through that golden instrument.

He didn't hear me so I tapped his arm. His eyes popped open.

"What are you listening to?" I shouted.

"Heaven on earth." He pulled off his heavy earphones and fit them on me. The sound of fast-paced, swing saxophones swirled around me. Two of them dueled in show-off riffs. I felt my feet starting to slide back and forth as if they had a mind of their own.

George grinned. "Pretty great, huh?"

I nodded. "What is it?"

"'In the Mood' by Glenn Miller—the best of swing. I'm working on arranging this for marching band. Emma's choreographing a routine for the flag corps to go with it, where the girls will flip their flags under and over each other like a gauntlet."

I listened a little longer. It was impossible not to sashay in time with that music. "But George, isn't this music kind of old-fogey stuff?"

"Whaaaaaat?" He grimaced and cocked his head with that I'm-giving-you-a-chance-to-redeem-yourself look. "You need some music education, little sister!"

He pulled the earphones off me and started flipping through a pile of CDs that he'd burned for himself over the years. George is totally retro. I think he likes having little discs of song like Daddy's enormous vinyl collection. As George searched, he preached. "'In the Mood' is the best of the best—those musicians have true skill, real courage. There's no remixing, no machine-made effects, no melodramatic dance videos." George was getting pretty worked up. "Back then it was just you and your instrument, man, standing there bare, slicing yourself open and letting the world watch your heart ache with each beat. Music should be an outcry, Ariel, not some sterile, sound-engineered mediocrity."

"An out-what?"

He sighed big and stuck a new CD into the player. "Here, try this." He plopped the headphones back on me, none too gently. I heard men singing in tight harmony, a bouncy baritone voice imitating the sound of a musician plucking the strings of a big ole bass: *Dom-dom-dom-dom-dommmmm . . .*

George shouted over the music. "It's doo-wop, early rock 'n' roll."

I listened and couldn't help smiling at the easy-bounce beat and the lead singer's sweet plea for his darlin' to "come go" with him. Suddenly the voices stopped, the singers started clapping rhythm, and a bluesy sax took the lead, dazzling up the melody with twisty runs of notes. "Yeah, yeah! Go, go!" the recorded voices encouraged him.

I put my hand to my ear and leaned into the sound, it was that good.

George seemed to know right where I was in the song. He nodded, eyebrows shooting up in what-did-I-tell-ya mode. "Nothing like a good saxophone."

At the time, I was struggling to learn cello because the school orchestra director said I had the brains for it. Classical music is ennobling, head-in-the-clouds beauty. (Theoretically anyway—once you get good!) This stuff was plain old delight.

"Hear that guy singing like an instrument rather than using words?" George asked.

I nodded.

"Okay, Ariel, this is what's so dope about music. That guy's white. The other guys are African American. The Del-Vikings was one of the first racially integrated music groups—before the Civil Rights Movement. They didn't care about the color of your skin as long as you could play. Music can overcome everything, change everything—that's what I love about it. Understand?"

I didn't, but I nodded anyway.

"Okay, here's a last one for you. Try some Springsteen. Talk about outcry. And listen to the saxophonist when he comes in—he brings the wail to Springsteen's poetry."

As the saxophonist started playing—raspy, raw— George handed me his precious alto sax.

"Go ahead—play!" I wrapped my lips around the

mouthpiece and honked.

"Yeah, yeah!" He laughed.

I honked some more. I'll be honest. I can't really play music that well. But George showed me I sure could *feel* it. And that opened a huge door for me.

George pulled the headphones off me and cranked the volume so we could listen together. He pretended to play harmonica along with Springsteen. I closed my eyes and danced as a song about keeping the faith in a promised land—no matter what—washed over me: *"The dogs on Main Street howl, 'cause they understand. . . ."*

Scene Four: "Come on, boy, give me twenty more."

George was doing push-ups at the Army Adventure Trailer, tucked in between the Apple Blossom Festival carnival games. "Bust three balloons and win." "Toss a ball into any bowl and win a fish." Framed by stuffed bears, George was on the ground, at the feet of an army recruiter.

George had just finished leading his high school marching band in the parade, conducting while strutting backward and twirling a big mace baton so the musicians all the way in the back could see and keep the beat. While they waited for the judges to announce their choice for the Festival's best band, he and Emma strolled through the game booths lining Loudoun Street. They didn't seem nervous at all about the judge's decision. If I were them, I'd be as itchy as a squirrel. But they walked slow, holding hands, stopping here and there, smiling and nodding at people. A dozen band kids dogged them, tripping up over one another to get close, telling jokes that always started with, "Hey George, listen to this . . ."

I suppose the army guy knew a natural leader when he saw one. He'd called George over and preached on democracy and the American Way and our need to finish what we'd started in the Middle East. He challenged George to show him "what you've got."

George never stepped back from a dare, ever. He hit the ground immediately. Now his friends were chanting the count: 90, 91, 92 . . .

"That's right, boy; there's strong and there's Army Strong."

George's face was the color of a Red Delicious apple, but he kept pushing up and down.

The drill sergeant smiled. "That's great, son." He pulled George to his feet and clapped him on the back. "I can see a uniform suits you well."

Scene Five: "You've done what? Oh, George, for pity's sake. Think about this carefully." Daddy jumped out of his favorite wing chair as he spoke. George stood in front of the living room fireplace. He'd just told Daddy that he'd accepted a commission to West Point instead of going to a music conservatory. George had even visited our senator and asked for the required recommendation from a member of Congress—all without telling Daddy. That's how committed he was. That army recruiter at the parade had achieved his mission.

Crouching on the staircase, I was eavesdropping and watching their reflections in the big hall mirror.

"I have thought about it," George answered. "When I graduate, I'll be an officer, ready to lead."

"But why?"

"I want to serve my country. To keep our freedoms safe. To protect people who can't stand up for themselves."

"But there are so many ways to do that without risking getting yourself killed," Daddy argued. "Like what I do, for instance."

I swear it was the first time I ever heard George be rude. He snorted.

And that was one of the few times I'd ever seen Daddy get mad, really mad.

He started pacing as he talked, like he does in front of a jury. "Our government officials hyped the danger of Iraq's weaponry to get us over there to fight and so often have used responsible, idealistic boys like you to control the Middle East's oil supplies or as a political maneuver to distract from other things," Daddy's deep voice boomed.

George stood, waiting him out as Daddy kept going: "Americans have always championed human rights. But lately our elected officials have made some pretty inhumane choices, first in interrogation methods we used in Abu Ghraib and then in all-inclusive travel bans, keeping Muslims from entering our country solely because they're Muslim, even if they have family here. You're a fool, son, if you think our continuing to fight over there is solely about preserving freedom."

"I'm a fool?" George finally exploded. "What about 9/11, Dad? One of my first childhood memories is watching the Twin Towers and the Pentagon burn. I want to prevent terrorist attacks like those from ever happening here again. But that's going to take American soldiers being in those countries, protecting their citizens who want democracy. I want to help them push back against extremist fundamentalists who might—oh, I don't know—shoot girls who just want to go to school and learn. Don't you think that's preserving freedom?"

Daddy started to respond, but George kept rolling. "I want to fight for people to have equal chances no matter their skin color or gender or religion or where they come from or if they're poor." George paused, took a deep breath, and his voice softened. "It's what you always told us you were doing, Dad."

It was those words that made Daddy fall into his wing chair and cry as George turned and left the room.

Scene Six: Skip ahead a few years until last month. "What's that?" I'd asked nervously. The image of George on my computer screen had shaken and a shower of dust had fallen on him. He and I got to Skype once in a while through the army MWR center when he was in base camp. (MWR, if you're interested, stands for Morale, Welfare, and Recreation. No wonder they need an abbreviation, right?)

"It's nothing, honey, just the Taliban making itself heard. Don't sweat it," George reassured me, but he glanced over his shoulder into the dimness behind him just the same. He mumbled, "Yes, sir," and then looked back into the computer. He smiled at me, but it was a weird, forced smile. "Gotta go, A. If you run into Em, tell her I really miss her, okay?" The image snapped black before I could answer.

During his college years at West Point, I'd reassured myself that, surely by the time George graduated, the fighting in Afghanistan would be long over. It's crazy that we've been sending our troops there for almost twenty years now. Our government says American soldiers are supposed to just be training and advising Afghan troops. But I worry George and his Special Forces buddies sometimes slip out into the night for actual combat missions.

I reached out to touch the screen where my brother had been. Even though I loved to see his face, it scared me, too. It was always dark behind him, and so often I heard gunfire thundering in the distance, like a squall line of death gathering around him.

Being way up on a mountain all alone, remembering these things about George, finally brought on tears. I couldn't fight them anymore; I felt so lonely with my big brother gone. So, there on the hilltop, I buried my face in my arms and sobbed. No one was around to make fun of me for it, so I let fly. But when I started sucking in dirt from the ground as I heaved, I figured I'd better stop before I choked. I forced my breathing to slow to gagging coughs. Finally, I lifted my head to spit out soil.

That's when I saw the dog staring through the grasses at me.

Four

MY HEART RATE ABOUT HIT ONE hundred miles per hour. I knew I'd been blubbering, but that dog getting so close—without my hearing—was plain old creepy.

I stayed frozen, chin to the ground just like it was. The wind was swishing the veil of grasses open and shut, so my view was like a bad Wi-Fi connection: clear then not, clear then not. But a couple of things I could see for sure. The dog had enormous ears—sticking straight up, quivering with listening. His face was long and golden, his eyes outlined with thick black. His snout ended in black, too, in big nostrils twitching like crazy to get my scent.

Now, dogs are pretty much a way of life around here. The Master of the Hounds for our local hunt lives one farm over and breeds foxhounds. I'm about the only kid in the county whose mother says we can't have a dog because they're too messy. I mean, this is a place where muck boots lacquered with horse manure sit beside the back doors of most homes. So I used to spend a lot of time playing with my neighbor's puppies. Those hounds love to chase things, jumping and knocking into one another in a pack of clumsy loudness. They bay and bark and yap. You can hear them coming a mile away.

So I'd never seen a dog that quiet, that watchful, that still. I raised my head slowly to get a better look. The dog pressed himself even flatter to the ground. The poor thing was thin and covered in mud, like he had been on the run for quite a while.

"Hey, fella," I said quiet and easy.

The dog started trembling.

"Aaaaw, easy boy. I'm not going to hurt you." I sat up, sticking my hands in my pockets to check for leftover cereal bar—like an idiot. The dog skidded backward as fast as a getaway car from a movie bank heist.

"Oh no, fella! I didn't mean to scare you." I stood, holding out my hand. "Easy."

For a moment the dog hesitated. But then he turned, tucked his furry plume of a tail tight between his hind legs, and slunk toward the nearby woods. He whipped his head from side to side, scanning the landscape. He was a gorgeous German Shepherd, really kind of noble looking except for the dirt and burrs caking his fur. Every twenty feet or so, he'd stop and look over his shoulder at me. Like he was too scared to ask directly for help but hoping I could see the need, begging me to follow.

So I did.

Higher into the hillside woods we climbed. The itty-bitty path we took narrowed and grew brambly, clearly cut not by park rangers but by deer meandering through their territory. I was constantly getting caught up in thorny wild rosebushes. The dog would slow down and sniff everything, checking the perimeter, while I pulled the coiling branches off my jacket and pants legs. Then he'd inch onward. It was like we were out on some kind of combat patrol.

The woods grew thicker and darker, so I couldn't really see the sky anymore, but I could feel the weight of air changing, getting thick and charged. My asthma kicked in and I wheezed. I knew what it all meant—a storm was brewing in the valley and heading my way fast. But I couldn't stop following that dog.

Ten more minutes. The forest's shifting shadows darkened into eerie, and I got as jumpy as the dog. My hands were so torn up from thorns, I thought I might burst into tears again. At this point, I knew I'd never find my way back. Suddenly home seemed a wonderful place. I'd even be glad to see G-L-O-R-I-A.

"Stop!" I cried. "Where are we going?"

I know. It's stupid to ask a dog a question. That's how scared I'd gotten. Believe it or not, that dog stopped. He sat down and stared at me. Completely silent. No panting, no scratching, no whining, no nothing. The only sound was wind stroking the trees, their translucent leaves shimmering with the touch, like when a drummer brushes the swish cymbal of a drum set.

Then I heard something that made absolutely no sense. The dog cocked his head to listen, too. There it was again: *ping*, a resonating bell, and then *ping-ping-ka-ching-ching-ching* in an answering chorus of musical notes.

I don't want to tell the word I said—it would prove all the church ladies' opinions of me. At the sound of those little bells, I figured the angel Gabriel (or something from the other not-so-nice side of the biblical spectrum) was coming to get me.

Then to make it all totally Harry-Potter-Forbidden-Forest-like, the woods lit up in a flash. BANG—lightning hit something. A long growling rumble rolled around and around the hills getting louder and faster, like a gigantic loose cannonball looking for something to slam against and explode to smithereens.

The dog howled, an outcry that made my skin prickle and my heart pound. Then he bolted.

"Wait!" I shrieked. "Wait for me!" I thrashed after him. "Stop! Stop! Stop!"

Another flash of scalding light, then unearthly blackness. BANG. The ground shook.

"WAIT!"

Pushing through bushes, as desperate as if I was doing the breaststroke in floodwater, I belly flopped into a clearing. In front of me squatted a campground-style cabin, no lights, deserted, maybe. Wind chimes hanging from its porch roof swung wild in the accelerating winds. *Ping-ping-ka-ching-ching-ching*. Freaky as H-you-know-what.

The storm was getting vicious—fast. Fallen pine needles that had carpeted the clearing levitated and swirled in little cyclones. Trees groaned in the wind. Diving into a thicket on the edge of the opening, the dog crouched there, shaking, looking toward the porch. Like he was saying, "Hey, stupid, I found you shelter; go for it."

Crack-crack-crack-crack-BANG. More mortar-like thunder. Horror-movie, zigzag strobe lights. I scrambled to my feet to run for the cabin as the lightning streak flared.

But just as I neared the steps, the cabin door flew open. "Halt! Identify yourself!" A figure rushed out—gun first. I could see it glint silver in the storm-light.

I slid to a stop and fell back on my butt, shaking as much as that dog had.

Virginia is an open-carry state, meaning people can walk around with handguns on their hips, Wild West style. Half the pickup trucks driving around the mountains during deer-hunting season have an arsenal of rifles on their gun racks. So it's not like I hadn't seen guns before. And just like every other kid in the United States these days—since grown-ups can't seem to figure out gun control laws strong enough to help prevent these attacks—I've had to endure countless active-shooter drills to practice what to do if some lunatic showed up at my school with a souped-up rifle and duffle bag crammed with ammo.

Even so, coming face to face with a gun? Aimed specifically at me? That's another thing entirely. I about peed my pants.

Thunder moaned. The dog bayed like a wild wolf. Lightning flash-banged.

Then pitch-black darkness.

"Who's there?" the figure shouted again. "Come out where I can see you." Then it fired a shot.

I didn't wait to learn if that bullet went into the air simply as a warning. I flipped and started swimming along the pine needles, just as the storm-cloud dam broke, pelting me hard with gushes of rain.

*Crack-crack-crack-*BANG. The world lit up.

"*Dios mío!* It's a kid. Oh my God. I'm sorry. I'm sorry," the voice called. "Stop!"

Are you kidding? I was getting the H-E-double hockey sticks out of there.

I heard feet running toward me. Barking. Dog teeth grabbed my pants and tugged backward. I flailed, sobbing. "Leave me alone!" A hand grabbed my arm. Suddenly I was jerked to my feet and dragged—kicking, shrieking, cursing—into the cabin.

The screen door slammed shut, and I faced the occupant, sure that my time on this earth was up.

The figure reached out and flipped the first switch it could reach—the outside porch light. Silhouetted in that beam was a small thin woman dressed in jeans and a camouflage jacket, her straight dark hair caught up in a long ponytail, hoop earrings catching the light. Backlit like that, I couldn't see her face. But what I was mostly looking at, of course, was the pistol she held.

"I didn't mean anything," I spluttered. "I was just

following the dog and the rain started and I saw your cabin and . . . and . . . Please don't shoot me."

The woman held up her hands in that universal sign of don't-worry-I-won't-hurt-you as she said, "I am so sorry. I was asleep and the storm woke me, and I thought . . . I thought . . ." She shook her head slightly. "I am so sorry to scare you. It's okay now." She started to lean over, and I backpedaled like a crab.

"No, no, it's okay. I promise." The woman put the gun on the floor and stepped away from it. Keeping her hands up, she inched toward a table lamp. She switched it on. "I'm Sergeant Josephina Martínez." She smiled. "Call me Josie. You're safe here. Let me get you a towel. You're soaked. And then we should see about getting your dog to come inside out of the storm." She nodded toward the clearing.

Having betrayed me by chomping down on my pants and helping this woman nab me, that dog was now sitting, all innocent and pitiful, in the downpour. I refused to feel sorry for him, though, because at that moment I wasn't completely sure if I was going to be shot or not. "He's not mine," I snapped, keeping my eye on that pistol.

Sergeant Josie looked at me quizzically but refrained from saying, "Then what the heck are you doing up here in a storm?"

She went into the bathroom and came back with a towel. I was shivering pretty badly by then so I snatched it and wrapped myself. I eyeballed her as she studied me.

This Sergeant Josie was nothing that I would have expected to find in a backwoods cabin. She was thirty-something, wiry, and looked like a total badass, Avenger-style action hero.

"What are you doing here?" I blurted out.

Sergeant Josie laughed. It *was* kind of a stupid question. I was the wacko out in a tornado-strong storm, after all. But she answered. "I needed some time in mountains . . . green mountains . . . peaceful mountains . . . to . . . to . . . I just needed some time." She shrugged. "Since we're sharing, what's your name?"

Because she'd laughed—usually my insolent tone brought a pretty self-righteous reprimand from adults—I answered without thinking about the fact that telling her my name was violating all childhood rules of not speaking to strangers. "Ariel."

"Really?" Sergeant Josie poked out her lower lip and nodded. "Ariel—spirit of the air." Thunder interrupted her, rolling and rattling the roof. The lights flickered. She paused, listening, before adding, "And of storms. Seems fitting."

I frowned. "Where do you get that from?"

"I've been doing a lot of reading up here." Sergeant Josie pointed to a waist-high stack of books piled against the wall. "I got that PBS Great American Read list and the BBC's Top One Hundred Books to Read Before You Die. Figured I'd homeschool myself a bit, since I skipped college to join the army. I just finished Shakespeare's *The Tempest*. There's a mysterious spirit in it that serves a sorcerer named Prospero, and she or he—it's hard to tell which—can gather winds and stir up terrible storms at the sorcerer's bidding and ride on 'curl'd clouds.' So if your parents named you for that play, that'd be tight."

I'd just read *Romeo and Juliet* in English class. I didn't know *The Tempest*. Well, the title figured. But my naming didn't have anything to do with poetry or magic or even me, really. "Mama named me Ariel because my big sister's favorite movie was *Little Mermaid*," I answered.

"Really?" Sergeant Josie made a face. "You mean the girl who gives up her voice to get a guy?" She made an even bigger what-the-heck face. She thought a moment. "I'm going to think of you as Prospero's Ariel instead. Pretty cool to have a name that's for a spirit who can ride the winds, don't you think?" She smiled reassuringly. "Now, we really should get that dog inside. I'm worried about lighting strikes. You know that lightning can hit ground and the current can travel right to where a person or dog is standing and kill them, right? That's why you go inside."

She leaned over so I could see her face up close and judge the sincerity of her words. "That dog did help me drag you in out of the storm. He's smart. And protective. You owe him, I think." She held out her hand to help me up.

I took it, ignoring all my misgivings. After all, with Sergeant Josie I wasn't a cartoon character, a titillating bit of church-lady gossip, an embarrassment, or an ignored nothing. I was a wind spirit.

Five

AS SERGEANT JOSIE'S HAND CLOSED ON mine, I winced and yelped. I'd forgotten how bloodied I was with scratches.

She turned over my hand to see where the brambles had torn open my skin. She even pulled out a tiger claw–sized thorn from my arm. "Those cuts need doctoring." Sergeant Josie led me to a wooden table and sat me in a chair. "I'm going to open the door. Maybe the dog will just come in on his own while I bandage you."

She propped open the screen door and whistled sharp and commandingly. Nothing. "It's all right, boy." She softened her voice and backed away slowly. "Nothing but friends in here. Come. When you're ready." Picking up her gun, she unloaded it, and shoved it in a bureau drawer before coming back with a medic-worthy first-aid kit.

She cleaned and wrapped my gashes in minutes.

"Are you a nurse?" I asked.

"Nope." She shook her head. "Just needed to know how to quick-bandage." She put away the gauze and glanced at the door. "I think you're the one who needs to call him. He obviously feels some connection with you."

"I haven't even petted him."

She shrugged. "The military uses that breed of dog because their instinct is to protect and defend. That kind of dog chooses his people. And then is incredibly loyal. Much better than people in that regard." Sergeant Josie crept to the door and leaned against the wall to look out. The rain was still gushing like a full-force fire hose. "He's crawled closer. Come look but move slowly so you don't frighten him."

I tiptoed to her. In the downpour, the fur of that poor dog was plastered to his body. He was squashed flat to the ground, his nose practically touching the bottom step, desperate for someone to notice and invite him in. "Do you have any treats?" I asked.

Sergeant Josie smiled. "There you go. Thinking like a dog-handler." She glanced over her shoulder to the kitchen part of the cabin. "I have some ham."

When she put a plate on the floor with a few cold cuts on it, the dog immediately raised his head.

"Pull back. Give him space."

We backed our butts into chairs. We waited. Rain pounded the cabin roof.

"Come on, boy," I murmured. A body could drown out there.

Finally, I could see a twitching nose on the top step, then paws, then his head on the edge of the porch.

"Don't move," whispered Sergeant Josie. "Encourage with your voice."

"That's it, fella. Come on," I called.

The dog wormed its body onto the porch, trembling all over. It about broke my heart seeing how scared he was.

"Come on. That's it."

He started inching, belly to the ground in that Special Forces commando crawl of his, leaving a trail of wet, he was so soaked. A little more. Closer. Closer. Oh, he was almost to the door when he flattened his body again, only raising his snout to sniff and snuff . . . sniff and snuff. Drool oozed out and hung in slimy ribbons from his mouth. I'd have been pretty grossed out about it, except I knew that meant he wanted that ham—bad. But he didn't move. Just sucked in smells like a crazed, furry vacuum cleaner.

"Why won't he come?" I whispered. I turned to look

at Sergeant Josie. Her eyes were welled up with tears—not what I expected from a gun-toting, dystopian-novel action heroine.

"I'm wondering if . . ." She broke off, swallowed hard, and her tears were gone. "Have you heard of the military K-9 units, the MWDs they use for special operations?"

"Sure," I answered. "Military working dogs, right? For the 9/11 anniversary last year we read in school about the one they took on the Osama bin Laden raid. His name was Cairo." I remembered because I'd been amazed a dog would parachute out of a helicopter strapped to his handler. How loyal and brave is that? Evidently hundreds of dogs have been deployed in Iraq and Afghanistan. I kept meaning to ask George if he knew one.

Sergeant Josie looked pleased.

Okay, score one for me, I thought.

"Working dogs are very special," she continued. "They search for IEDs that soldiers can't see. Such a lofty-sounding term—improvised explosive devices," she muttered, "like they're some clever school science project. They're devious, snake-in-the-grass, homemade bombs packed with things like nails to tear people's flesh open. The enemy hides them purposefully where people walk all the time. Civilians. Our soldiers. They don't know pain is lying in wait for them at their very next step. Not until they trip the unseen wire. Then BOOM!"

I jumped a little at the BOOM. The dog whimpered.

"Sorry." Sergeant Josie sighed. "But dogs like that, trained right, will sniff out those booby traps. They save dozens of lives every week. One of the places insurgents plant bombs is in doors. So K-9s have to check every entry point before their soldiers step through them. Smelling every inch. Just like this dog is doing." She pointed toward him. "When those dogs determine it's safe, they let their handlers know. That's when our troops kick down doors. Or throw noisy flash-bang grenades through entrances. Which can't help but scare the poor dog, even after intensive training. So working dogs always associate doors with danger." She glanced over at me. "Where did you find this dog?"

"In the hills, maybe a half mile from here? I don't know: he led me on a pretty wild-goose chase."

"And yet, he brought you here." She looked back to the dog. "To shelter in a storm."

"You're not thinking this dog is military, are you?"

She shrugged.

"That dog? Cowering like a terrified cottontail rabbit? He's so afraid of everything. He couldn't be . . ."

I stopped short. I'd seen my own brother's nervousness

when we Skyped. Would George, full-of-life George, marching band–confident George, be like this when he came home? I felt sick with the thought.

"Yes, that dog." Sergeant Josie shot me a look that reminded me this woman had a gun handy. "Wouldn't you learn to be afraid if you spent months in-country and whenever you walked down a road you had to worry about a homemade bomb exploding beneath your feet? Or about being shot by a sniper you can't see? Or that the child waving so friendly at you could be strapped with a suicide vest?" She was getting seriously worked up as she talked. "Having dozens of lives dependent on your being suspicious, your head on a swivel, on super-alert every single moment? That dog would have pushed himself to do his duty over there. No matter what. But how do you come back down from that to normal civilian life? The problems would have started back home . . . *after.*"

She bolted to her feet. "You people just don't get it!"

I fell off my chair. The dog backpedaled like mad. But he stayed on the edge of the porch, watching. It was hard to tell for sure over the thunder that was still rumbling around, but I thought I heard him growling. Was the growl *for* me or *at* me? Could I run away from this woman, out the door, and survive?

I must have looked terrified because Sergeant Josie

apologized about a hundred times in ten seconds. She held her hands up again and backed herself to the wall, away from the bureau with the gun, away from me, away from the dog.

"I'm sorry, Ariel. Ever since returning from my tour of duty . . ." She stopped. "I'm working through some stuff. Leftover stuff. The army docs say I've got PTSD. You know, post-traumatic stress. Me and almost everybody else I know that shipped out with me. It's not like I'm crazy or anything. Just a little . . . jumpy." She closed her eyes and breathed in—a long cleansing gulp—and then blew out slowly. She opened her eyes. "Listen, I can help you with that dog if you want. I used to be a K-9 handler in Afghanistan."

"My brother is in Afghanistan right now," I squeaked, still pretty freaked out by her.

"*Vaya con Dios*, man." She murmured and made the sign of the cross. "You want to get that dog to come to you out of the rain?"

I nodded.

"You'll need to train him to know what is safe. If he really was a working dog, he'll need to learn what is appropriate behavior now that he's back home." She gave me a kind of crooked, self-conscious smile. "He and I can learn about that together." She crossed her arms and gazed at the dog for a long moment.

"The first thing is to get him to trust you enough to come through that door. To convince him, you must be firm, Ariel, but still empathetic. Patient but not coddling. Just like a good mother loves her child enough to sometimes say no and then takes it when her kid screams at her about it. Right?"

A truly good mother? "I wouldn't know," I answered, I guess with a little too much spit in my tone because Sergeant Josie's eyebrow shot up in that aha-I just-learned-something-about-you expression that teachers get sometimes. But she only said, "Ready?"

I sat inside the cabin, by the open screen door as she instructed, right behind the plate of ham. Because he seemed so petrified of the threshold, we put two more plates of ham outside on the porch, leading in a trail toward the door. The closer he got to it with nothing bad happening to him—and getting a treat to boot!—might help him trust that the door was safe, she said.

"We'll have to be patient," she added. "This may take awhile. Remember that comforting him when he's frightened will make him think you're pleased when he's afraid. Instead, you need to show him that what really pleases you is when he follows your cues."

As soon as I positioned myself just inside with the final plate of food, the dog's tail began to wag, tapping the porch floor. *Thump-thump-thump.*

"That's right, boy. Come on," I urged.

Thump-thump-thump.

"It's easy-peasy, fella." I picked up a piece of ham and wiggled it.

Quivering, the dog eased himself up to a crouching, hesitant walk. One paw, then the next, he crept from the edge of the porch, where he had retreated, back toward the door.

"Good job." Sergeant Josie whispered encouragement. "Carry on. Just like you're doing."

I nodded. "It's okay, boy. Come." I held up the ham again. The dog made it to the first plate and inhaled the meat. Then he wriggled backward a foot or so, licking his chops. He stayed rooted.

"Why doesn't he come to the next plate?"

"Hmmmm." Sergeant Josie thought a moment. "Some handlers use a technique called treat and retreat. He may be repeating something he learned—meeting a challenge, getting a treat, and then retreating to let go of the tension of the situation. Give him a minute."

After what felt like a hour, but I know was only ten minutes or so, the dog slow-motion crawled forward to the second plate. With a slurp, that ham was gone. He flattened himself to the porch floor and studied me.

"It's okay, boy. Come on. It's safe. I promise." I nodded as I spoke and smiled. I dangled the ham again. "Come on."

Never taking his eyes off me, the dog crept forward again, inch by painful inch. I held my breath as he tested the opening with a paw and a thousand sniffs. But he sat down and hung his head. Stalled.

I lowered the treat, disappointed and defeated. Maybe he didn't like me. Of course, I thought. Who did?

Sergeant Josie frowned. "Don't give up that easily, Ariel. Don't expect success to be handed to you. Try again."

I held a piece of ham up to my own my nose. "Mmmmmm. Smells goooooood."

The dog lay down. He started sniffing and snuffing again—so hard he might have sucked in any fly within a mile.

"It's all right, fella, really it is." But he didn't move.

I'd love to tell you that it was my *empathy* that made me keep working. But in truth, the rain was so awful, I was stuck there in that cabin and couldn't give up and stomp away in a huff. So I kept at it.

I pretended to eat the ham. The dog whined.

I made kissy noises at him.

The dog just farted—talk about bombs.

Very slowly, so as not to startle him, I put my hand through the door to show him it was safe, but the dog howled as if to warn me off.

Finally, since there seemed to be nothing to do but wait for his courage to take hold, I started humming like I used to do to make myself relax when I was afraid of the dark at bedtime. And the thing I hummed was a slow, sweet melody that George had played on his soprano saxophone. I used to hear him practicing it downstairs when I had been sent off to bed for the night—usually early and in disgrace for some misdeed. It was a solo with the jazz band for a big competition. George practiced it over and over. I had fallen asleep listening to that tune dozens of times.

The dog's ears twitched. He started doing that gentle little whimper-whine dogs do to get a person's attention, like musical breathing. Then—wonders of wonders—he started wriggling toward the door again.

I can't really describe how painful it was to see a dog so terrified of a door. But I kept humming and he kept coming, squirming along until finally he was halfway across the threshold and his huge tongue shot out like an anteater's to lap up a piece of ham from the plate beside me.

"Good boy!" I sang.

Piece by piece he wolfed down those last cold cuts. Then he hurled himself into my outstretched arms. He licked me so much, I thought he'd wipe my nose right off my face. Soaking wet, smelly, slimy with mud—that mess of happy dog rolling all over me was the best hug of my life.

Six

AFTER THE RAINS CLEARED, I LEFT for home. Sergeant Josie offered to keep the dog overnight. Tomorrow she and I could figure out what to do next. Like finding out if he belonged to someone. I was so attached to him already, I asked if we could forgo that bit of truth telling. But she'd have none of it.

She told me how to find the main path to Sky Meadows and even pulled out an old-school compass to give me. "Due southeast," she said. Turns out her cabin was only a couple hundred yards from the main trails, which made me all kinds of irritated with that dog, given our submarining through briar patches. But my aggravation melted as I left and the dog hovered just inside the door watching me, like he could hardly wait for me to return.

I wondered how Sergeant Josie would get him out the door to relieve himself that night and then back inside over that threshold. But I figured if Sergeant Josie survived Afghanistan, she knew what she was doing. I certainly had obeyed her—she made so much sense when she spoke. Like telling me, *IF* the dog didn't already belong to someone, I needed to name him. To give him personality and a listen-up-fella identity to use with the cues we would need to train him.

I was considering calling him Oscar—since it was Oscar Mayer ham that brought him to me. But I wasn't so sure that was heroic sounding enough. As I hiked down to where I'd ditched my bike, I ran through names from novels I loved: Merlin . . . Arthur . . . Lancelot . . . Aslan . . . Reepicheep . . . Caspian . . . Martin . . . Matthias. . . Gorath . . . Harry . . . Hagrid . . . Ron.

No, no, no, no.

When I finally got home, dirty and worn out, I went straight to the library to look in books for name ideas. And guess what I found?

Gloria and her boyfriend making out on the couch.

Now, I have to admit that I did spy on them and on George and Emma sometimes. I don't think I'll ever forget the sight of George and Emma the night before he had to leave for deployment. They were slow dancing on the old fieldstone patio awash in the moonlight, long after everyone else had gone to bed. He was playing that gorgeous song "Stand by Me." Hearing the line, "No, I won't be afraid, just as long as you stand, stand by me" about broke my heart, thinking on his going off to battle. I'm sure it did Emma's. Their romance was so pretty and . . . well, romantic.

Gloria and Marcus? Not so much.

"Hey there!" I chirped from the door. Yeah, I know, that was kind of a jerk move, but I was still steamed at G-L-O-R-I-A from the morning.

They fell onto the floor in an avalanche of old *National Geographic* magazines that Daddy must have been reading and they hadn't even bothered to push aside.

"Ariel, you little . . . ," Gloria shrieked.

I thought the word she used next was right shocking for a Blossom princess.

Marcus, on the other hand, burst out laughing. "Hey yourself, Ariel."

Here's the thing about Marcus. I like him. You can see yourself, he's got a sense of humor. And he sure isn't boring. Maybe that comes from his being homeschooled in a double-wide by a mama who's a psychic and a daddy who's a Revolutionary War reenactor named Morgan—in honor of Winchester's Continental Army general, Daniel Morgan. As a result, Marcus approaches everything with a sense of destiny and fanfare.

For instance, you can hear his car coming all the way up our hickory-lined lane blasting "Crazy" by Patsy Cline, that tragic blues-and-country crooner from Winchester he claims to be related to. And he's got sayings like "carpe diem" tattooed all up and down his arms.

("Carpe diem" means "seize the day." I looked it up.)

He's also dead honest. Like now. "Do me a solid, Ariel," he said, getting serious. "Don't tattle, okay? It'll get Gloria in a world of trouble. It's my fault. Your sister is just so darn beautiful and I'm so in love with her, I can't help kissing her."

Now, how many guys do you know who'd be that upfront about how they feel?

So as much as I'd love to get Gloria in trouble—Mama *hated* her dating Marcus—I promised I wouldn't tell. And I keep my promises.

He kissed Gloria on her head and got up to leave. Grinning at me, he said, "Come on out to the car, Ariel. I've got something to give you."

I walked out with him, thinking with some sadness that my promise probably wouldn't do Marcus much good. Just the other morning, in fact, when he had texted, Mama snatched up Gloria's phone and deleted Marcus's message before Gloria got to read it. "You don't want to be limiting yourself to the likes of him,

Beautiful," she'd said. "I grew up with boys like Marcus. Believe me. No matter how nice they are, no matter how sexy that country rebel-with-a-cause image is, in the end, it's going to be near impossible for them to amount to much in this world. Too much stacked against them. At the Festival, you'll meet all sorts of university boys. Marines will escort you at the parade. You want to keep your eyes"—she cupped Gloria's chin and tilted her face up so she was paying close attention to Mama's words—"and your options open."

Listening to Mama had made my skin crawl. Her prejudice against her own childhood community and her quest to turn G-L-O-R-I-A into a total "It Girl" reminded me of the evil stepmother in Cinderella, with that character's conniving to elevate her own daughters with the prince. Mama's comments also made me wonder if Daddy had been "an option" in Mama's eyes—which would way validate the icky stuff the pearl-ladies said about her. I didn't like to think about it.

In the back of Marcus's Mustang was the huge pizza-slice costume he wore to dance around street corners to advertise a local pizza joint. He reached in and pulled out a wad of coupons to the place. "Here, take these."

"You don't need to bribe me, Marcus. I won't tell."

He frowned. Lighting a cigarette, he let it droop from his lips so it popped up and down as he spoke. "It wasn't a bribe, just a thank-you. Share them with your friends." He pushed them at me again.

"I don't really have friends, Marcus." I thought about the boy with the big gleaming smile, who sat behind me in Civics. But he probably didn't even know my name and definitely didn't need to be getting pepperoni stuck in his braces.

Marcus frowned again. "Why not? A smart girl like you?"

"Maybe I'm too smart for my own good."

"That stinks."

"Yeah, I know," I answered.

Since I wouldn't take them, Marcus tossed the coupons through the window of the front seat. They landed on a copy of devotionals for deer hunters and a really fat book titled *Don't Know Much About History: Everything You Need to Know About American History but Never Learned.* He breathed in his cigarette and considered me a moment.

"You really should stop smoking, Marcus. It's terrible for you. And it stinks up everything. Mama will know you were in the living room because of the smell."

"Darn it," he muttered. He threw the butt to the

ground and squashed it with his heel. "Now see there, Ariel? That was being a good friend." He stuck out his hand. "I'd be proud to consider you one of mine."

"Really?"

He nodded.

So I shook his hand tattooed with a swallow. And I knew that I would do my best to make him feel better if things went sideways with Gloria because of Mama. To be honest, Gloria liking Marcus, and her braving Mama's disapproval, had helped me like her, a little anyway.

Still, Marcus being so nice to me made me think I should warn him not to count on things too much. It came out all geeky, of course. "Hey, Marcus, do you know that your tattoo, 'carpe diem,' is from a Latin poem? It starts with 'seize the day'—which sounds all hopeful— but it ends with 'putting as little trust as possible in the future.'"

"Shoot, girl, that's pessimistic. You gotta have belief in the possibilities every tomorrow promises. Otherwise how do you get up in the morning?" He winked at me as he got in the car. "Hey, here's a thought. You know I work at the animal shelter on Saturdays, right?"

I nodded. Marcus worked hard. He was mainly a handyman, able to fix most anything with a screwdriver, duct tape, and some paint. He and Gloria had met when

Marcus was fixing gutters and rain rot around our house. He was constantly being called by the county's new residents, those SUV drivers with their Bluetooths and bumper stickers bragging on their honor student kids. I swear they do Google searches to hire help for just about everything except screwing in new light bulbs. So Marcus was able to piece together a decent enough living.

"Why don't you come pick out a dog?" he suggested. "We've got a bunch of really nice ones in right now."

I ached to tell him about the German Shepherd—the dog I was already starting to think of as mine—but I didn't trust Marcus that much yet. So I just spoke a truth: "Mama won't let me have a dog."

"Say what?" He thought a moment. "Well, come on over this weekend, and you can help me brush them. I try to get them out in the yard to exercise and clean them up some. That way they have a better chance of being adopted when people come in."

Wow—a real invitation. Like a friend might make. Things were definitely looking up! "Okay, thanks!" I smiled.

"You know what, Ariel? You've got a real sweet smile." He grinned, turning on his car's engine with a roar. "See you Saturday." With that Marcus drove off, his tailpipe smoking and "Take Me Home, Country Roads" wailing from his Mustang.

I went inside to pick up those magazines. They were scattered and jumbled, their covers turned up and corners squashed. Gloria never picked up after herself— ever. You can't even see the carpet in her bedroom, it's so layered with her panties and T-shirts and dresses and sweaters she's taken off and just dropped. I didn't really care about Gloria getting busted. In fact, it kind of would have made my day. But I didn't want Marcus to be barred from coming to the house now that we were officially friends.

It was pretty reckless of Gloria to be sucking face with Marcus indoors. But Mama *never* sets foot in the library. It's Daddy's sanctuary. The corner where his desk is smells of Daddy's tweedy jackets and leather briefcases. But there's nothing museum-stuffy about our library. Those books are well-loved companions.

Once, I found notes scribbled all over the margins of O. Henry's really beautiful short story *The Gift of the Magi*. The one about the woman who cuts off and sells her hair to buy a pocket-watch chain for her husband for Christmas, not knowing he's sold his precious watch to buy special combs for her luxurious, long hair. In delicate, perfect cursive were these English teacher–smart comments: "Exquisite sacrifice and irony," "If only all love were this true," "Mythology of selflessness."

When I asked Daddy who made those notations, he kind of twitched as he stared down at the pages. "It's your grandmother's handwriting," he said softly. "She earned her doctorate in English literature from the University of Virginia. One of the first women allowed to do that, you know."

"No, Daddy, I didn't. I don't know anything about her." That's when I realized that I'd seen nothing anywhere in the house about the woman who'd raised him.

Daddy fished around in his top drawer and pulled out a black-and-white photo of a woman in a formal fox-hunting coat, sitting tall and straight on a horse, surrounded by foxhounds. Her face was in profile, turned away from the camera mostly, so all I could really see was a long nose and thick, even frizzly hair caught up in a chignon under her velveteen riding hat. "She was brilliant . . . witty . . . could recite entire poems. She was stern, exacting, but unwavering in her devotion to those she cared for . . . a quick-flash temper . . . a magnificent rider." Daddy said all that, strangely hesitant. "She always made me think of women warriors—like Cleopatra. Terrifying but wonderful."

Daddy took the photo back, looked at me kind of funny, like he was going to say something else. But instead he tucked it into the desk's top drawer and left the room.

I've pulled the photo out a bunch of times since then to look for clues about what made my grandmother as righteous and fierce as a woman warrior. So far I could find nothing in her appearance, other than her straight back and the aura of self-confidence her posture hinted at.

But there wasn't time for that today. Daddy would be home from work soon and head into his retreat before dinner. I started stacking the magazines Gloria and Marcus had dislodged, and I was pretty happy doing it. I do love a pile of *National Geographic*s. It's like dozens of windows looking out on the entire world all at once. Daddy must have had serious trouble sleeping the night before—court cases he's really worked up about keep him awake sometimes—because there were about twenty issues lying there, new ones and old ones.

Sitting in that pool of covers, I couldn't help lingering over photos of coral reefs and translucent fish, mysterious places like Stonehenge, exploding volcanoes, robed men riding on camels, close-ups of bug-eyed lemurs. I definitely couldn't resist reading about the mama panda cuddling her baby. People all over the country are constantly tuning into the National Zoo's Panda Cam, so how can you blame me?

But it was another article in that issue that really grabbed me. It was on the joy and the healing powers of dance. I was completely enthralled by stop-action sequences of ballerinas, ballroom dancers swirling in glittery gauze, and a photo that really rocked me: a dog standing on his back feet dancing with a lady in pink sequins and tap shoes. They were competing in Dog Dancing. "Musical Canine Freestyle" is the fancy name. I kid you not—there are national competitions all over the world for this. The article quoted a judge who said, "With the right piece, the dog lights up. Its tail wags harder."

I thought about how my humming had helped that traumatized German Shepherd beat back his terror and come through the door to me. Music must be a powerful incantation for him. It certainly was for my brother—what made George feel "invulnerable."

Tomorrow afternoon, I was going to play lots of tunes for that dog at Sergeant Josie's cabin. I closed my eyes and envisioned juking with him. I was flying happy in my imagination when Gloria completely crashed me. Talk about a buzzkill.

"Hey, Loser," she sneered from the doorway. "You ever

sneak up on me like that again and I'll find a way to embarrass the hell out of you somewhere when it counts. Understand?"

I peeped open one eye. There G-L-O-R-I-A stood, neat and primped, makeup perfect, her naturally wavy hair ironed flat in a long sheen of gold. As if she could humiliate me any more than she already did with her snipes and shunning.

Mama called to her from the front hall. Sweet as syrup, Gloria turned and sang back, "In here, with Ariel. She's been into Daddy's magazines again, and I was just telling her she better pick up her mess."

Gloria checked her cell phone, giggled, and texted something back to one of her thousand friends. Without even looking my way, she threw one last barb at me. "And don't kid yourself about how nice Marcus was to you today. It's only because of me. Next time he's here, I'll tell him not to bother."

Mama shouted again, fussing about being late for the princess meeting.

"Coming!" Smiling dreamily, Gloria flounced away.

That's when anger boiled up in me as fast and dark as a squall line gathering along the Shenandoah. And the idea—an idea fit for a wind-spirit, tempest child who could conjure storm clouds and might be destined to go to H-E-double hockey sticks—came to me. Right then and there I knew that I was going to teach that dog to dance. Music would set him free of fear and elevate my soul out of nobodyhood.

Then he and I were going to crash the Apple Blossom parade to steal some of G-L-O-R-I-A's thunder.

Seven

THE *NATIONAL GEOGRAPHIC* ARTICLE WAS OVER a decade old, so I turned to YouTube to get the current scoop on dog dancing. Typing in those two little words took me to a whole new universe. Dachshunds to Great Danes danced with their trainers to ragtime, hip-hop, and rock 'n' roll. I traveled to competitions all over the world and witnessed crazy-good performances.

One man pretended to be Charlie Chaplin, that silent movie guy with the little mustache and bowler hat, twirling a cane and waddling like a windup toy. His collie pranced along beside him in perfect step. Then the collie seemed to get full of himself and took a flying leap to knock Charlie flat on his back. Charlie's legs sprawled up into a V. The collie jumped through the man's legs, did break dance–like spins, added that scraping thing dogs do to kick grass over their poop, and finally hopped around on his back legs like a boxer does after KOing his opponent. The crowd guffawed with laughter.

But the routine I hit over and over again was a lady and a golden retriever with Rapunzel-gorgeous fur. The dog glided back and forth under his handler's legs as she walked. He cross-stepped in perfect rhythm. He bowed as she kicked her legs over his head. He sashayed backward, shifting directions as flawlessly as she did, and spun round and round, vaulting off the floor, his tail whip-wagging the whole time. At the end of the routine, he jumped into her arms and covered her with kisses.

I wanted my stressed-out, bedraggled German Shepherd to feel that kind of trust and companionship, to move with that kind of happy abandon. I wanted to be like that lady. I couldn't see her up close to know for sure what her face was like, but dancing with her dog, she was beautiful. She was graceful. And she'd had eight million views!

If I could teach him to dance, maybe people would talk about what I had created, rather than what I looked like or what *they* thought I *might* become given *their* definition of worth. Maybe they'd even stop comparing me to G-L-O-R-I-A.

I fished around YouTube to find how-to instructions. I quickly learned the choreography involves a lot of "heel work," treats, and hand signals, plus breaking the routine into little pieces, practiced over and over again before linking the segments together. I could do that.

The first step was finding music to suit the dog's movements and attitudes. Well, I thought, my phone was crammed with over a thousand songs. With all those choices, I'd find something that German Shepherd would like. My real problem would be keeping my mind on school the next day until I could climb the hills to Sergeant Josie's cabin.

That didn't go so great. I flunked an Algebra test. I'd completely forgotten about it, I was so excited about dog dancing. So getting half the problems right was a decent accomplishment, I thought. But the teacher didn't. She gave me an F *minus*. What's that all about? If you flunk, you flunk; there's nothing below that, except to rub it in.

But she was *that* kind of teacher—the overly ardent kind who seems personally insulted if her students screw up and gets really impatient with them, which borders on ridicule, if you ask me, when done in front of the whole class. Maybe she'd been a teacher's pet all her life and now that she was on the other side of the desk didn't know how to give positive feedback rather than get it. Maybe she was just socially inept. But she sure was messing with my one little shred of self-esteem. It meant a lot to me that I was in the "gifted and talented" section, taking high school–level math as an eighth grader. Six kids had washed out and left her class for "regular" math, looking like that shell-shocked German Shepherd as they did. I'd been terrified I might be next.

Normally I would have stewed on that test failure for days and called myself all sorts of names. But as the school bus belched its way out of the parking lot at 2:25, I put in my earbuds, turned on music, and tuned out my own noise.

Kids from the county's most rural areas go to my school, so our buses cover a lot of geography. It can take forty minutes for mine to make it to my stop. It's some beautiful territory, though, full of lush rippling hills, sun-danced ponds, and fields of horses chasing each other just for the fun of it. So I don't mind the trip. Normally those views soothe me as I head to the rocky world of home.

But that day I was saved instead by Sara Bareilles playing piano and singing "King of Anything," her defiant rejection of people imposing their opinions on her self-concepts. She makes it real clear that no one should try bossing her around. But she's not all mad about it, so the song is totally catchy. Come to think of it, I discovered her on YouTube, too, singing on a bus with marching band musicians playing in the back seats. The video makes me think of George. So I can listen to the song over and over again as a kind of pep rally when I need to lift my mood.

It plays for 3:23 minutes. That meant I could listen to it twelve times before I stepped off my own bus that afternoon at my driveway. I divided it out in my head (to get 11.8343-something). See, Ms. Math? I know what I'm doing!

When I got home, I dumped my books, pulled out my bike, and headed for the hills. At Sky Meadows, I started climbing, happy and excited. But up on those trails, I got all turned around trying to refind Sergeant Josie's cabin. I began to wonder if I had just dreamed the whole thing when I heard the wispy tinkling of wind chimes, far-off, faint and haphazard. I followed the little stream of bell-song. That's how quiet the world is up there on those hills, how much the wind picks up a sound, cradles it, and carries it right to you—if you're listening.

The music led me straight to the clearing. As I neared, I could see Sergeant Josie and the dog together on the cabin steps, soaking in the sunlight that sifted through breaks in the forest canopy. They both had their faces lifted. Josie was smiling, eyes closed. The dog was sitting on her feet, sniffing in every smell the wind was dangling around him. They both looked so hushed, so peaceful, so renewed.

She'd even brushed him clean of burrs. I felt a stab of jealousy. Was she going to turn out like G-L-O-R-I-A, hogging the attention of anyone I hoped would love me? But when that dog saw me, he dove off the steps to jump all over me, licking my face and nosing my hands for treats.

"Hey," I greeted Sergeant Josie as I walked to the porch, the dog hip-hopping all around me.

"Hey yourself," she answered as she stood. "Come on inside. I made cookies. My mom always had cookies waiting for me after school. I think they're still warm."

Cookies? I don't think I'd ever before had a plate of warm anything waiting for me after school. I almost drooled like the dog when she offered me a plate full of sweet vanilla sugar cookies.

I broke off a piece to give him, assuming he was still beside me. But the dog had stayed outside, sitting sentry, looking in through the door. "He won't come in?"

"No. I got him out last night, and he hasn't left the clearing. But he hasn't come back through that door again either."

She waited until I had downed the second cookie to bring up finding out if the dog belonged to anyone. I almost spat the cookie back out at her when she did. "I called the local shelter to see if anyone reported a missing shepherd and no one has. He's obviously been traveling on his own for a while. But we should still have him checked for an identity chip. If he's a Military Working Dog, he'll have one. But"—she held up her hand to stop my protest—"we need to get him to trust us first. Right now, I don't think I could get him into my truck to take him there without re-traumatizing him. And that would totally blow his ever trusting you."

I perked up on the word *you*.

"You don't want him?" I whispered.

Sergeant Josie shook her head. "My dog died." She hesitated. "That recon went all wrong. He . . . he was . . ." She shook her head again, harsher this time. "I don't want another dog." She looked out the window, clenching her hands as she did. But I could see the shake in them—that leftover stuff she said she suffered. Sergeant Josie took in a deep breath and turned back to me. "Besides, it was you he picked in that storm."

In a torrent of hope—like sunlight spilling through a cloud hole—I jabbered out my idea about dog dancing and the parade. I left out the revenge finale of sticking it to G-L-O-R-I-A. I was smart enough to realize that as kick-butt as she obviously was, Sergeant Josie followed an honor code that probably wouldn't be into that kind of thing. But the idea of that dog waltzing free and happy—she liked that a lot.

"First thing to do," she said, "is to get him to come through that door again. Thought of a name yet?"

I shook my head.

"Maybe the music he likes will tell you a good one. Ready to begin?"

Between Sergeant Josie baking me cookies and the fact it took only two for the dog to ease himself back through the door, the afternoon started off promising. But that's where easy ended. For an hour, no song got him dancing—no matter how much Sergeant Josie or I liked it.

I started with cellist Yo-Yo Ma and singer Bobby McFerrin performing a lively version of "Hush Little Baby" because Yo-Yo Ma is a hero of mine, being mutual cellists and all. I turned hopefully to the German Shepherd. But he just started barking out the window at a squirrel.

Changing to music Daddy and George loved, I picked Ella Fitzgerald singing "Cheek to Cheek." That ballroom dance song had been good enough for Fred Astaire and Ginger Rogers—probably *the* most famous dancing pair *ever*—to waltz to in one of their movies.

But the dog lay down and went to sleep.

I tried Rufus Wainwright's "Hallelujah" (Yeah, okay, I did first hear it in the movie *Shrek*—that movie where even a green ogre can find love and acceptance, which made it a favorite for me.) The dog actually snored! I guess that song does sound a little like a lullaby.

So I pumped up the beat and tried something thematic: "Who Let the Dogs Out" by the Baha Men. That German Shepherd rolled over and sneezed like I'd insulted him.

I threw up my hands.

Sergeant Josie laughed. "Try Pharrell Williams's 'Happy.' It always makes me want to dance."

That sure got me up, bebopping around the dog. He didn't move, not a whisker. How is that possible? I decided to try an amazing pianist-singer I'd recently discovered, who had that soul-rattling outcry George talked about—Alicia Keys. Her "Wait Til You See My Smile" made the German Shepherd sit up and pant like he understood the lyrics and was trying to smile at me. But no dance.

"Hmmmm. May I try?" Sergeant Josie spun through her playlist. "Here's my favorite singer, Alynda Segarra.

She's from the Bronx. She said what got her through a tough growing-up were the weirdos and the poets, the rebellious women and the activists—what people in power consider the riffraff, so she named her group Hurray for the Riff Raff. Isn't that clever? These days she's writing a lot about Puerto Rico—that's where I'm from. I think you'll like her."

Sergeant Josie pushed "Living in the City." During the refrain, "Well, it's hard, it's hard, it's hard," that dog put his paw on Sergeant Josie's knee, all empathetic and worried.

"Aww, it's okay, fella." She patted his head. "Maybe it's too soon for political resistance music for him. What else you got?"

I switched to girl-power anthems: "Roar" by Katy Perry, Aretha Franklin's "Respect," "Fight Song" by Rachel Platten, Carrie Underwood's "Nobody Told You," and "Defying Gravity" from *Wicked*. His ears twitched and I swear he nodded his head in rhythm, like he was thinking right hard on those lyrics. But he was too serious about it to get up and strut.

I flopped into a wicker armchair, feeling totally defeated. I'd run through dozens of songs. I swung my legs up over the chair arm and kicked them back and forth. Sergeant Josie didn't reprimand me for it. She also didn't start pushing a bunch of advice at me like most adults would have or complain that we'd just wasted a lot of time. She picked up an old frayed book to read.

Even though I would have resented her telling me what to do next, I was also annoyed that she wasn't, because I was totally out of ideas. "What are you reading?" I admit my tone was pretty why-aren't-you-saving-me cranky.

Sergeant Josie simply held the book up so I could see Homer's *The Odyssey*—that ancient epic poem about Odysseus finding his way back home to Greece after the Trojan War.

"I have to read that next year when I'm a freshman. It sounds really boring."

"Really?" She looked up and a bit of chill ran through me at her expression. "You think soldiers trying to find their way back home after a long war is boring?"

"N-n-no," I stammered.

Sergeant Josie just stared at me.

I squirmed.

She waited.

I cleared my throat.

She sighed, relenting. "It's actually a wonderful story, Ariel—dead accurate—about journeys . . . resilience . . . self-discovery. Piecing yourself back together after your world has been torn apart. Or when you've seen way too much death." She looked back down to the pages.

The dog rolled over and put his paws over his face.

Okay, I may be slow to understand people sometimes, but I'm not stupid. I got why she liked it. I felt my stomach turn over with anxiety. When I said something that annoyed Mama, I paid for it with days of her barely speaking to me. When she did, her voice reeked with disdain. After your own mother has acted like she's totally repulsed by you, it's hard not to panic about the possibility of being rejected by a new friend when you goof up. I really liked Sergeant Josie. I didn't want to lose her.

I changed the subject—fast—hoping that would save me. "That's quite a lot of books you have there," I said awkwardly. Exactly the kind of statement that made kids my age walk away from me. You'd think I'd learn.

"Mmm-hmmm."

Well, at least she didn't sound like she'd just seen a cockroach or something. I got up and looked at the titles—*The Great Gatsby, Pride and Prejudice, The Outsiders, The Grapes of Wrath, The Sun Also Rises, Jane Eyre, Lord of the Flies,* and *1984.* Stuff I was going to read in high school.

Some of them I'd already read and loved: *The Secret*

Garden, The Giver, the Harry Potter and Narnia series, *The Book Thief, Anne of Green Gables,* and even *Charlotte's Web.* "Hey, I know these. Why are you reading these as an adult?"

Sergeant Josie looked up. "They're on those PBS and BBC lists of books everyone should read."

Really? PBS thought kids' books were just as good as adult ones? All right! I'd be sure to throw that at some of my peers who called me a nerd for reading so much.

"How many have you read?" I pushed.

"About half."

"Like them so far?"

"Most, yes."

Clearly, she was still smoldering or trying to ease down from being annoyed with me, so I let it alone. I knew better than to worry a wasp nest. I also had no idea what would be the right thing to say, so I stared out the window, absentmindedly thumbing through songs on my phone. Without really thinking about it, or I guess subconsciously wishing George was there to help, I pressed "Sir Duke," Stevie Wonder's tribute to big-band legends and the "king of them all," Duke Ellington. George had arranged it for his marching band, weaving in a wicked cool drumline interlude.

Well, that song wasn't more than a measure or two

into its opening trumpet and saxophone fanfare when the German Shepherd woke up, sat up, and lit up. The tip of his tail started slapping the floor, in that hint of happiness dogs give right before they really start wagging and squiggling all over with joy.

Rushing so the magic of the moment didn't break, I cranked the volume right where Stevie sings:

Music is a world within itself
With a language we all understand . . .

I jumped up and swayed with the music, waving my arms in time to the beat. "Yeah, boy, good boy," I cheered.

The shepherd started circling me, prancing, barking, his tail going round like a propeller. Sergeant Josie clapped her hands to the cymbal beat. I was so excited, I did a victory lap, skipping around the cabin. The dog followed, yip-yapping, his feet catching at my heels.

We were feeling it "all o-o-o-ver" just like Stevie Wonder was singing, just like I had when George let me honk on his saxophone and introduced me to the soul-filling rapture of music.

Moving with those exuberant lyrics, barking along with those trumpets, the dog didn't even notice that we passed right by that scary door three times.

We had found our music. And his name: Duke.

Eight

I'M GLAD I DIDN'T KNOW HOW hard teaching Duke to dance a complete routine to music was going to be or I might have given up before we even started.

Achieving an effortless-looking performance takes a heck of a lot of *effort!* Getting Duke to heel—following right by my side, matching his steps to mine—was easy. As long as I didn't try going through that threatening door, of course. He also sat and stayed on cue. So right from the beginning, we had a couple of decent dance moves. He'd sit and let me skip around him. He'd trot along beside me as I walked in serpentines. But beyond that? We had an awful lot of learning to do and boring, frustrating, oh-my-God-make-it-stop repetition.

Each day after school, I biked and climbed the hills to Sergeant Josie's cabin. I'd show Duke a move and then practice it over and over and over.

It was like learning to play the cello. Before I had been

able to even attempt an easy piece, I'd had to learn how to finger the notes, how to string them together without stumbling, how to stay in tune as I played. It'd taken me two months to eke out "Twinkle, Twinkle"—a baby song that only had six notes in it. Two months!

We had only four weeks till the parade.

I started with simple things like a spin. Honestly, if you clutch a piece of bacon, any dog is going to follow your hand, nose to your fingers. So I would circle my hand in a big O, Duke pirouetting to keep that enticing bacon aroma in his nostrils. "Good boy!" I'd cry after each circle. Then I'd switch the direction. "Good boy!"

Eventually I could get Duke to do four tight spins in a row without holding anything in my hand, just pointing and rotating my wrist. *Then* a treat and "Good boy!" I did the same to get him to weave in and out through my legs as I walked.

Sergeant Josie must have fried up ten pans' worth of bacon for those two tricks alone.

At night, I worked on creating the actual dance routine. Suspecting Gloria would make fun of me if she saw, I worked in our old dirt-floor basement, where I could dance out of sight. George had sometimes played hide-and-seek with me there. But mostly the basement had been my private stage. I don't know how many times

I'd acted out fairy tales or Nancy Drew mysteries down there with my stuffed animals when I was a kid. Just me and my Winnie-the-Pooh under the spotlight of a bare bulb hanging next to the jelly cellar.

The cellar shelves were stacked with damson plum preserves my grandmother had jarred—the only thing in the house I ever found that I knew for sure she had made. Those and the scribbled responses to literature. The jars sat, their sweet contents probably poisonous by now, relics of the time our place had been a working estate with cows and fields of vegetables. We still have a thick grapevine in the back arbor that bears fistfuls of ink-dark grapes. The bees and birds enjoy them since Mama keeps us supplied in grocery store jelly. Which explains why nobody ever came down looking for jam. Only George had ever thought to search me out in the cellar, wondering where I was when I disappeared for an entire day.

So I about jumped out of my skin the night Daddy called, "Hey, Ariel. I was in the hall and saw the light under the door. What are you doing, sweetheart?" He was sitting halfway down the open-rail stairs, like he'd been there for some time watching me walk, spin, lean over to shake Duke's imaginary paw, repeat.

I yanked off my earphones. Stevie Wonder sang into the room.

"'Sir Duke!'" Daddy brightened. "Great song!"

"Yeah." I couldn't think of anything else to say. It's stupid, but I felt as weird as if Daddy had caught me smoking a cigarette. I turned the music off.

"I was worried you were listening to something god-awful like rap."

"Actually, Daddy, a lot of rap and hip-hop songs are really good. You should listen to *Hamilton*; everyone else in the country has! The composer, Lin-Manuel Miranda, won that prize for it—you know, the one you think is so important—the Pulitzer."

"Pshaw," Daddy answered. We went silent, starring across a several-generations gap in music. He tried again: "Were you dancing?"

"Yeah."

"Are you choreographing something for school?"

"Yeah," I lied.

I could have kicked myself. Here was a rare chance to actually talk to Daddy without Gloria interrupting. But I was just too embarrassed. Or maybe Daddy and I had chatted so little lately that I had no idea how to have a real conversation with him.

"Our own little Martha Graham!" He smiled at me.

"Who?"

"The lady choreographer who pioneered American

modern dance. Mother took me to see her company when the Kennedy Center first opened. We used to have season tickets to all sorts of theater performances in DC when I was your age. I loved doing that with her." He stopped and frowned. "Didn't your mama and I take you to see Martha Graham's *Appalachian Spring* when you were little? I remember our splurging and spending the night at the old Willard Hotel next to the White House. You were all excited about getting room service—a club sandwich and a chocolate sundae. Remember?"

"No, sir. That must have been Gloria."

"What?" Daddy rubbed his nose, the quirky thing he did when he was getting uncomfortable with a situation. "Are you sure?"

I certainly was! That kind of attention had always been spent on G-L-O-R-I-A, the anointed family flower worth tending and coaxing into bloom. I kept hoping she would just go away—like George had to college—so in the void I might capture some of Daddy's interest. But the laser focus on G-L-O-R-I-A had only flamed into full-scale floodlights when she stayed home and went to our local community college so she could take private acting classes with drama professors from Shenandoah University. Come to think of it, part of the real iciness between Gloria and me started when I asked, if she had actually done her homework during high school, could she have gotten into the university itself and acted in their drama conservatory's really wonderful plays.

"Well," Daddy tried again, "I know your ballet class went into DC to see *The Nutcracker* because you dashed around in a tutu pretending to be a sugarplum for weeks afterward. Remember doing that?" He laughed fondly, taking off his glasses and polishing them with his handkerchief. When he put them back on, he saw that I wasn't smiling in response.

"That was Gloria, too."

Daddy seemed genuinely startled. He stared through me, and I knew he was rifling through a mental file cabinet of memories, trying to find some envelope that applied to me. He looked pretty distressed.

I decided to help him out. "We went to the National Zoo a bunch of times with George."

"That's right!" He perked up. "We saw Ling-Ling."

I didn't have the heart to tell him that particular panda had died before I was born, that he must be remembering a trip from when George was a baby. For a few moments, Daddy's face clouded. I knew he was thinking of George.

But Daddy kept trying. I'll give him that. He switched topics again. "You'll be going to high school in the fall."

"Right."

"Bet boys will call all the time to ask you to dances."

I was seriously beginning to wonder if someone had slipped something funky into his coffee at work. "I don't think so, Daddy."

"Sure they will, honey." He thought a moment. "Do you know how to do the pretzel? You know, when you go under your partner's arm, turn around and end up on his other side, all while keeping your eyes locked." He smiled. "It's very romantic. "

"Eeeew. No. No one dances holding hands anymore, Daddy."

"That's sad, don't you think?"

Actually, I agreed with that. The slow swing dance that he and Mama did looked like a lot of fun.

"Well, let me show you the box step, then. I want you to be able to slow dance without getting too close to a boy. Not my little girl."

"Daddy!" I was totally mortified. My face broiled again at the image of the boy with the big smile and the gleaming braces holding me in his arms.

Daddy came down the stairs. I was so stunned by the attention, I let him put my left hand on his shoulder and take my right hand in his left. He sidestepped us to the right (pause), back (pause), left (pause), back, in a neat little square, then again. He hummed as he moved us.

Somewhere from way back in my past, my memory called up Daddy's deep baritone voice singing: "Oh my dar-ling, oh my dar-ling, oh my daaaaarling A-ri-el." Suddenly I remembered standing barefoot on his shiny loafers as Daddy danced me around and around, substituting my name for the song's Clementine. I could hear our long-ago laughter. I remembered the feel of his swinging me, my being almost parallel to the ground, and then the big bear hug he'd give me before putting me back down, dizzy and hiccupping with happiness.

Oh, I had forgotten. I'd been so balled up in being mad and disappointed with all the emphasis on G-L-O-R-I-A that I had forgotten these kinds of moments between us. And they had existed—*before* George left, *before* Gloria's and Mama's disgust with me and mine with them had hardened up.

Daddy kissed me on my forehead. "You know, Ariel, you are growing into a graceful young woman."

"Really, Daddy? You really think so?"

He held me out at arm's length. "Of course, honey." He cocked his head at me—the same way George did when he was questioning something I said as being way harsh on myself. I realized for the first time how very alike they really were.

"Thanks, Daddy."

He was about to say something else when through

the floorboards we heard: "Eddieeee? Eddieeee? Time for *Wheel of Fortune!*"

No, No, NO! Not now. Just a few more minutes, I silently begged.

Daddy shrugged, almost like he was acknowledging on what a short leash she keeps him. "Your mama got all the word puzzles right last week—every single one— and she's thinking of auditioning for the show." He climbed the stairs and paused at the door. "Coming?"

"No thanks," I answered. What I really wanted was to plead with Daddy to not leave. But in my disappointment, I simply defaulted to snarky. "She hates it when I guess the puzzle before she does."

"Eddieeeeeeeeeeeeeee!" Mama was annoyed now.

Daddy smiled down the stairs at me, then was gone. Like music turning off.

I stood on the bottom step, trying to memorize the feel, the melody of the last few minutes, like a hymn of possibility. Maybe, just maybe, if he saw Duke and me dancing *my* choreography in the parade, Daddy would actually remember which of his daughters he was watching.

Nine

Subject: vacation plans

From: jazzlver

To: AplusGirl

Hey A,

Can't wait to be with you in Rehoboth. I'll be playing Whac-a-Mole until I see you. First thing I'm going to do is eat a month's worth of Thrasher's fries. It'll be a cakewalk on the boardwalk—LOL! Big hug, G

Saturday morning, I sat in front of my computer, rereading the last email I'd gotten from George. To anyone else, his words would make no sense. But I understood George's code. Leave it to him to be so clever while maintaining army secrecy. We weren't meeting in Rehoboth, although I wish. No, talking about our family's favorite beach and Whac-a-Mole was George telling me he was going out on reconnaissance to look for Taliban insurgents. And the bit about the amount of boardwalk French fries he was going to eat meant he'd be on the move for four weeks or so.

Bottom line? George was letting me know he wouldn't be able to Skype for a while but not to worry. He expected the patrol to be easy, "a cakewalk."

I tried not to be baby-selfish, but I was really disappointed. I wanted to tell him about Sergeant Josie and Duke and dog dancing. And get his advice. To be honest, I was starting to have a lot of doubts about the whole thing.

Not dancing in general—that was coming along well. I'd choreographed a pretty sweet routine, and Duke was getting it. I was even training him to shake his head and lift his front paws—alternating left, right, left, right— in time to Stevie's beat, barking right on cue with the saxophones on the verse about big-band legends like Louis Armstrong, Count Basie, Glenn Miller, "and the king of all—Sir Duke." *(Bark, Bark!)*

No, I was just getting cold feet about crashing the parade. How mad would everyone be, I wondered. Could I get arrested? Would Daddy represent me in court if they threw me in jail? What if Mama or G-L-O-R-I-A convinced him to let me stay locked up?

Maybe the whole idea was just too crazy. Besides, what made me think I could create something anyone would be interested in watching? And dancing in front of people who thought I was ugly and a troublemaker and destined for H-E-double toothpicks? I'd just be giving them ammunition to make fun of me.

Plus, I'd been so obsessed with Duke and dog dancing, I was screwing up big-time in school—the only place where I'd always done well. I'd managed a D plus on my latest Algebra quiz, which I suppose was a step up from an F minus. But that sure wasn't saying much. Ms. Math had even asked me if I thought I belonged in her class. There it was, the question of my life: did I really *belong*?

I kicked at a growing pile of dirty socks. I managed to stub my big toe bad on shoes hidden beneath.

"You are so stupid, Ariel!" I screamed at myself.

Dropping to the floor, I rubbed my throbbing toe, the pain shutting me up for a minute. Sitting there in my laundry reminded me that George was always asking us to send replacements for the socks his combat boots wore thin. So I eased down my panic and switched to thinking about stuff that really did matter—like George being in Afghanistan and out on patrol, where all sorts of truly bad things could happen.

Well, if I couldn't Skype, I could write a letter and send it in a package of stuff he always needed. Every month, I organized a family box to send George. The post office was good about making sure flat-rate packages found their way to service people pretty fast, even if they were out in the field.

I went down to the front hall closet, where we kept shipping cartons and the required customs forms. I knew Daddy had already written his monthly note and been collecting things to send George. On his desk, I found his sealed letter atop a pile of toothpaste, gummy bears, batteries, granola bars, lemonade crystals, the latest edition of *Rolling Stone* magazine, and toilet paper. I gathered them up, knowing Daddy was still in bed. Mama insisted that Friday be date night. If their evening included going to see a movie, that meant driving thirty minutes of back roads to Leesburg or Winchester. On those nights, they never got home before midnight, which had to be way late for a sixty-four-year-old guy.

Opening the box, I put in Daddy's items first. George had asked me to send stuffed animals that he could give to Afghan kids when he was on patrol—out where tribal villages had next to nothing, not even running water.

Back when they were all the rage, Mama had purchased a gazillion Beanie Babies, thinking she'd make a fortune reselling them. But when the *Wall Street Journal* reported a while back that no one wanted the little creatures anymore and they were only worth fifty cents apiece, she threw them into the trash in a fury.

Their little faces had looked so sad in our garbage can, I fished them out. None of them are the ones that eBay is suddenly listing for ridiculous prices, so I was sending them to George a handful at a time. I dropped in an owl, dragon, snake, parrot, and bat. That pretty much crammed the box full.

My letter became a long one, all about Duke and the storm and Sergeant Josie and dog dancing. How hard it was. How excited I was. How much I wished he could see my choreography. How much I wished I could ask his advice. Here's the last bit of it.

You wanted me to find what would make me feel "invulnerable." Like music does for you. Maybe this is it? Maybe. It's kind of crazy, though, dog dancing. Right? But it makes me feel like Charlie and Sam and Patrick in The Perks of Being a Wallflower *at the very end when they finally found* the *tunnel song and they're zooming, driving in Patrick's pickup, and for that one precious moment, Charlie feels infinite.*

Thank you for telling me about that book, George. I wish I could be friends with those three characters.

Oh! I have a book for you. I'll send it, too. Swing. *I think you'll really like it. It's about a lot of stuff, but JAZZ runs through the whole thing. It calls Benny Goodman "the fixer . . . the sway and swoon," his music "melody in your steps" and "a chance to dance offbeat."*

Be safe. Please.

xoxo, A

I blew on the paper to dry the dumb tears I'd let drop onto the letter and then placed it and the book so they'd be the first things George would see when he opened the box. Balling up newspapers to tuck around the edges to keep things from sliding around, I chose sections I knew George would be interested in flattening out and reading. I was just about to tape it closed when I heard Gloria's alarm go off next door. Nine o'clock—that was way early for her on a Saturday. She must have a princess meeting, I figured.

Now, about the only thing G-L-O-R-I-A and I had ever agreed on was that our brother was Mr. Wonderful. It'd be a real jerk move on my part to send him a box and not ask if she wanted to include something. I started to tape the box up anyway. I sure didn't owe her anything these days.

But George has always been a good influence on me,

whether he's in the same room or on the other side of the world. He wouldn't ever be that nasty on purpose. He might think less of me if I were. Plus—as much as I worried that G-L-O-R-I-A might manage someday to turn George against me, too, if she got a lot of time with him—I knew his feelings might be hurt if there was nothing in the box from Gloria. So I forced my feet to walk across the hall to her bedroom.

Knocking, I shouted, "Gloria, you up?"

No sweet singsongy response from our Blossom princess. "What do you want?" she snarled.

"Want to put something in our box for George?"

I heard blankets being thrown around, then shuffling. Rubbing her eyes, Gloria pulled open her door. For someone who is so gorgeous most hours, she sure can look strange in the morning. To give herself soft curls, her hair was pulled up and threaded in and out of a headband. The updo actually worked, but she always woke up with her hair sticking out in tufts like a crazed chrysanthemum. Gloria still wears a retainer to keep her smile Hollywood perfect, so her teeth were rubber-banded. Her face was lathered with white acne medicine. And, I'm sorry, her big pink slippers with feathery poufs at the toes looked like clown shoes to me.

She seemed so put out by my standing there, I couldn't

help myself. I wrinkled up my nose and said, "You might need some more beauty sleep there, girl." Part of me meant it to be a joke, you know, teasing as if we liked each other, but it came out mean, G-L-O-R-I-A caliber mean. I deserved what I got next.

"As if you would know anything about beauty."

We glared at each other.

I shifted the box in my arms.

Gloria put up the truce flag first. Our half brother had that effect on her, too. Her tone was almost civil as she asked, "Did you say something about George?"

Following her lead, I answered with normal politeness. "Yeah. I'm going to mail our box to him today so it's waiting for him when he gets back from patrol. Do you have something you want to put in?"

She looked at me funny. "How do you know he's out on patrol?"

I figured George had emailed Gloria the same kind of message he had me but she just didn't get his code. "You know, the one about vacation plans."

"Vacation?" she interrupted. "The army lets George go on vacation? Where would he go?"

"He was being cryptic. Vacation obviously means patrol." I stopped myself from putting on the *duuuh* expression she and Mama always hurled at me. But I gotta admit I was feeling it.

Biting on her lower lip, Gloria asked, all weird: "He emails you?"

Her surprise set me off big-time. "What? You think he doesn't care enough about me to email me?"

Those turquoise eyes of hers—that everyone is so gaga about—bugged out as big as robin's eggs, I swear. But she didn't say anything. Which also was way weird. I had no idea what she was stewing on. But I could see she was thinking hard on something.

She turned slowly, like she was considering taking some jab at me. Or maybe asking another question? But then she stomped to her bureau, where she picked up a letter and, of course, her cell phone. She kissed the note and then held it toward me, without looking up as she scrolled through the text messages that were already coming in fast, one little chime after another.

I could see scrawled across the pink envelope: *Guess what? I'm a princess!* Biting my tongue to keep from making an obvious sarcastic remark, like "could you help me out here, Your Majesty?" I rattled the box to show her my hands were full.

Letting out a Hollywood-worthy sigh of exasperation, Gloria looked up long enough from her phone that she could drop her letter into the box. It landed on *Swing*.

"What's that?" she asked.

There was an edge to her voice now. Her usual impatience with me, I assumed. But ask me about a book and I am going to open up, hungry. "Kwame Alexander writes really cool verse novels. All razor-sharp, to-the-soul poetical. This one he co-authored with a lady named Mary Rand Hess, and it has a lot about jazz. George and I have been reading books and talking about them while he's in Afghanistan. I thought George would like this one since he loves big-band music so much."

Again, Gloria looked at me all weird.

I kicked myself for being so honest and earnest, making me all *vulnerable*.

"You and George are such nerds." She said that strangely quiet and thoughtful. But then, as if some other thought hit her upside the head like a harsh wind, she shifted to G-L-O-R-I-A grade nasty: "Nobody likes know-it-all girls. Or book geeks. No wonder you don't have any friends."

She started to close the door, but a new text popped up on her cell phone. She froze. "What is this?" She held it up so I could read a text from Marcus: *Tell Ariel I'll pick her up at 9:30. We have some dogs to beautify.*

He remembered! I hadn't been sure Marcus really meant the part about taking me to the animal shelter.

And I'd figured Gloria had told him to ignore me just as she'd threatened. I grinned. As big as a princess.

That really infuriated Gloria. "What does he mean about beautifying dogs? Where are you going?"

"Just to the animal shelter. He asked if I'd like to help clean up some of the dogs so they look more adoptable when people come in."

Again, a momentary, out-of-character quiet. Then she gave a dramatic who-the-heck-cares kind of shrug. "I couldn't see Marcus today anyway. I'm busy with a dress fitting for the parade. I won't be able to spend much time with him at all during the Festival. Then after that . . . ," Gloria trailed off, and gave a very different kind of shrug. For a moment she looked sad almost. Definitely pensive. Then, just like before, a sudden swing back to that mean-girl, princess-up-on-a-high-horse voice: "So he'll have time to do a little charity work with you.

"And I'm sure *you* can be a help to the *dogs* there. After all"—Gloria leaned toward me and looked me in the eye to slap me with that dehumanizing, sexist, old-time slur for a woman someone thinks is unattractive—"it takes one to know one."

She slammed the door in my face.

Did I say I was having second thoughts about sticking it to G-L-O-R-I-A at that parade?

Ten

G-L-O-R-I-A DIDN'T EVEN BOTHER TO COME down to say hello to Marcus when he arrived at nine thirty sharp. He was disappointed, I could tell. But he looked over my shoulder up the staircase only a couple of times before refocusing his gaze back on me as we talked. Marcus was also incredibly nice about agreeing to run me by the post office to mail George's package. He said he had an errand he needed to do, too, and both stops were right on the way to the shelter (even though I knew for sure the post office wasn't).

"Your parents know where you're going, right?" he asked as I came out the front door behind him.

"I didn't have a chance to tell them last night," I fibbed. I didn't want him to know I hadn't mentioned it because I hadn't believed he'd actually show up to take me.

"Hold on." Marcus put his hand up like a school

crossing guard. "Run back in and tell them."

"Daddy's in the shower. Mama's still asleep."

"You need to write them a note, then. Make sure you turn on your phone so they can get ahold of you if they need to."

I frowned. I tended to light out from the house without anyone ever wondering where I was going. I know a lot of my classmates would think that was dope, like I was being granted some big freedom. But I've always suspected that my family just didn't care enough about me to wonder where I was. "They won't want to get ahold of me, Marcus. They never do. Besides, my cell loses its charge fast. I only turn it on when I need to use it. I need a new phone, but Mama says I have to do a month of folding laundry and dinner dishes to earn a replacement." That was a month of her basically not having to do much housework.

It was Marcus's turn to frown. He herded me back through the door. "Write a note. We'll give them my cell number. Tell them they can call me if they need to find you."

As I left the scrap of paper on the front hall table, tucked up under the old engraved silver vase, I wondered if anyone would notice it.

When we got to his Mustang, Marcus took George's

box from me to put in the back seat next to an unopened Jesus Toaster. Then he held my door open for me—like I was a grown-up lady or something. As I slid in, I was impressed with how neat and clean the car was. No cigarette odor at all. One of those pine tree air fresheners—red to match his car—hung from the rearview mirror along with the tassel from his high school graduation cap.

He got in and reached over to turn on the radio. "What type of music do you like?" he asked, as thoughtful as if I were a guest in his home.

I couldn't help it. No one was ever that nice to me. I blurted, "You have such good manners, Marcus."

The dark look he gave me made my stomach flip-flop.

"Think because I live in a trailer park and not some old fancy house like yours that I can't have good manners?"

"Oh no, Marcus, I didn't mean that."

"Yeah, you did."

He turned the ignition, and the engine revved with a pop out the exhaust pipe. He drove out our long drive slow as a turtle, like maybe he was considering not taking me after all. I kept quiet, afraid I'd ruined things, just like I almost did with Sergeant Josie and my dumb comment about *The Odyssey*.

Since Mama and Gloria never apologized for any of

the mean things they said to me *on purpose*, it was hard to know how to say I was sorry, especially when I did something wrong completely by accident. Apologies with them also turned into ambushes, a chance for Mama and Gloria to bombard me even more from atop their self-righteous high hills. When you get that beat up, any sane person avoids stepping into the same situation.

But I'd just managed to insult this totally sweet guy. I glanced over at him nervously. Marcus reached down to shift gears, his *carpe diem* flexing as he pulled back the stick. Right. Just seize the moment. "I'm really sorry, Marcus. All I meant was that I was grateful for how gentlemanly"—oh God, that probably wasn't the right word either—"I mean . . . I mean . . . how thoughtful you were being. To me. I . . . I really appreciate it."

Now Marcus looked over at me, with a small frown on his open, honest face. "It's okay, Ariel." He picked up speed. "I better hurry if I am going to get you to the post office and me to work on time."

He made several turns on the road before he spoke again. "Look, Ariel, my dad was a total tool until he was saved. Now he's always preaching scriptures at me. A lot of it goes right past me, but his faith has done a lot for him and I never forget one lesson: treat others the way you'd like them to treat you. That's really what manners are about, aren't they?"

He added, "Besides, Mom is forever reading my fortune. She says my palm tells her that I'm going to be a famous world leader. She named me after the Roman emperor Marcus Aurelius, after all. If I'm going to live up to all that, I suspect I need to have some diplomatic niceties."

Marcus drove without saying anything else for a bit. "I don't know about being some big-shot world leader. But I am going to start taking classes at the community college with Gloria in the fall. If I do good enough . . . I mean *well* enough . . . , I can transfer to Lynchburg or Liberty or Longwood. Or if I really get my act together, maybe JMU. From there, who knows, maybe even . . . " He paused and said quietly, "Maybe even law school."

Oh, Marcus. I could see what he was thinking. He was banking on the belief that, if he became a lawyer, Mama would have to accept him. Daddy would, but it was going to be a lot harder for Mama. She seemed so all-fired determined to put serious distance between herself and the trailer-park world she came from that I couldn't see her ever allowing Gloria to settle down with such a reminder of her past. I'd heard Mama say as much when she'd deleted Marcus's text.

But all I said to him was, "That's great, Marcus. You'd

be a great lawyer." And he would, too.

He smiled over at me. "Why live if you don't have dreams, right? I've almost got the first year's tuition saved up. Makes digging out rain-rot and shoveling dog poop at the shelter and humiliating myself in a pizza outfit seem worthwhile."

Mulling over Marcus's hopes sure put into perspective my stupid tendency to doubt myself. He was right. Everyone should have dreams—even if they seemed small ones. After all, if this country boy, whose father was a reformed alcoholic and his mother a fortune-teller, could hope to go to law school . . . if a blind man like Stevie Wonder could teach himself to play piano and sing to thousands of people in an audience he couldn't see . . . if a dog could have the guts to sniff out bombs and jump out of a helicopter for the love of his handler . . . and if my brother could worry about giving toys to children while he tried to survive a war zone . . . then surely I could manage my simple little goal of dancing with a dog in a small-town parade.

Reenergized, I rolled down my window and breathed in—deep. It was one of those gorgeous spring days in Virginia that gives you all sorts of hope in this world. Soft cushions of clouds decorated the deep blue sky. Redbuds, those spindly little trees that have to stretch and contort to catch drops of sunlight under the wide shade of tall trees, were erupting in strings of purple star-blooms. Wild lilies were just beginning to bloom orange along dark-ivy embankments. A breeze carried the perfume of opening lilacs as kindly as a good Southern hostess might offer a refreshing glass of sweet tea.

"Beautiful morning," Marcus murmured as he gazed at the horizon. Rather than tuning into the radio, he decided to slide a CD into his car stereo. A crisp bluegrass guitar filled the car and a raspy male voice sang, "Never woulda hitchhiked to Birmingham if it hadn't been for love. . . ."

Marcus started tapping the beat on his steering wheel.

"Hey! I know this." I brightened. "It's an Adele song!"

"Well, she covered it. It's Chris Stapleton's song."

"Really?" Gazing out the window, I listened. When the singer belted the refrain with the same kind of to-the-bone melancholy Adele did, I thought aloud, "Wow! He gets the ache as good as she does. That's surprising."

Marcus laughed. "Shoot, girl. Think women have the monopoly on hurt feelings?"

I turned and looked at him, startled. "What?"

He glanced my way and then, refocusing on the road, said in a low voice, "Think guys don't cry?"

I was so blowing this ride. I didn't know what to say in answer to that. Anything I said had the distinct chance of being W-R-O-N-G.

Marcus smiled. "Tell you what, Ariel. Look up Chris Stapleton singing 'Sometimes I Cry.' Deal?"

"Okay," I answered.

He nodded. "Okay, then!" He started singing along with his CD, reaching over to nudge my shoulder. "Come on, now!"

I joined in. Shout-singing in the ain't-it-the-truth drama that a real heartache song offers, we turned up a gravel road. It narrowed and climbed as Marcus's car crunched along its gray stones and black hulls shed by the walnut trees sheltering it. Right as the song ended we pulled in front of a whitewashed clapboard cottage with a faded green tin roof. A very old woman was sitting in a wicker rocker on the shade porch.

"I'll just be a second," Marcus said. He reached into the back of the car to grab the toaster. As he got out of the car, he called, "Hey, Beautiful. How's my best girl?"

Oh my, how that lady lit up. "Marcus? That you, sugar?"

I have to be honest. She wasn't exactly what I'd call beautiful. Her face was as furrowed with wrinkles as the bark of an old oak tree. Her scraggly white hair was held up with a mass of rainbow-colored butterfly clippies that sort of made her look like a porcupine. And dang, the woman had a pretty noticeable mustache—even from where I was sitting I could see it. But the smile she gave Marcus as he leaned over and kissed her cheek was drop-dead gorgeous.

"You feeling okay today, Miss Dottie?" He handed her the toaster.

"Oh, lookee, lookee." She hugged the box to her big broad bosom. "You got it!"

"Yes, ma'am. Didn't I say I would?"

"Best way to start the day—with the Lord's face beaming up at me from my toast. Thank you." She took Marcus's hand and swung it back and forth like a child might in the playground. "Come break bread with me soon. Promise?"

"How about when I bring your groceries this week?" He knelt so he was eye level with her. Only then did I realize she was having a hard time seeing much beyond her arm's length because of the way she brightened when he came into her clear view. "But you have to promise me a spoonful of your fair-winning honey with my toast. Got any left?"

"For you?" She smiled and patted his face. "You know it, sugar."

"How're your bees doing? Started coming out yet?"

"I heard them yesterday," she pointed to a dogwood starting to bloom by her porch.

"Good. I'll check the hives for you when I come back."

"And I'll have that box of donations ready for you then, too."

Marcus stood. "Gotta get to the pound. Want me to set up the toaster before I go?"

"No, angel, I can do that myself. You go on now." She blew him a kiss and waved as he got in the car.

"Who's that?" I asked as we drove away.

"Maybe my best friend in the world." He hesitated a moment. "I don't know how much you know about him, but my daddy got hurt on the job. Hauling trash in Winchester." Marcus's expression tightened. "Did you know trash-collecting is the fifth deadliest job in the United States?"

"No," I murmured. I was ashamed to admit I'd never much thought about trash collectors before.

"Well, it is. And there wasn't any workers' comp when it happened to him. I'm told that Daddy had always been a work-hard, play-hard kind of guy. So it's not as if he wasn't acquainted with the bottle before. But he hit it hard after he got hurt, to cut the pain. He could get . . ." Marcus stopped. "Let's just say Miss Dottie found me hiding in her woodshed more than once. And she must have taken me in and stood between me and trouble—serious trouble—a hundred times."

He drove on, and I felt squirmy uncomfortable, not knowing if I should say I was sorry for what he was telling me. Some people don't like feeling pitied. I'd already been clumsy about his sense of pride that day, so I was afraid to screw up again. But I sure did feel sorry, even if I didn't say it.

He stayed silent. So I changed the topic. "What donations is she talking about?"

"Clothes for the apple-pickers. You know they come mostly from the Caribbean, so they don't always have warm enough clothes when they head north, following the crops. Daddy's been chasing out demons for people ever since he was born again. He was called in to their migrant camp once to help a poor old guy who was sure some ghost was after him in the orchards. Ever since, Daddy's been organizing drives for them.

"These days, so many of our friends are so mad about every last thing and blaming immigrants for our troubles that Daddy's having a hard time getting much of anything for the pickers. But Miss Dottie? She always comes through. I've never known her to turn away any stray soul or dog."

He kind of shook himself. "Speaking of which!" Marcus grinned at me. "Ready to do some dog beautifying?"

I wanted to tell Marcus that, if he'd wait for me to grow up, I would love him to the day I dropped. But instead I covered up my gaping at him and his kindness with asking, "Got any Springsteen?"

Marcus grinned. "Does a ladybug got spots?"

"My brother loves Springsteen. Especially his band's saxophonist."

"The Big Man."

"Who?"

"Clarence Clemons. The E Street Band's saxophonist," explained Marcus. "Springsteen called him the Big Man. Those two were like brothers. They played together for almost forty years. Isn't that something? So tragic that Clarence died."

"Oh no! I wonder if George knows. It'll make him so sad," I worried aloud. I felt my soul shudder—like a cloud of bad luck had passed over me—hearing that the saxophonist George so loved had passed away.

"I'm sure George knows, honey. Clarence died, gosh, almost a decade ago now." Marcus glanced over me. "You and your brother are close?"

A lump grew suddenly in my throat at the question. All I could do was nod.

"You look like you miss him."

I nodded again, pressing my lips together to stop their quiver.

Marcus thought a moment. "You ever heard Clarence's 'You're a Friend of Mine'?"

I shook my head.

Marcus pulled over and flipped through a box of CDs, saying, "The Big Man lives on in his music, Ariel. That's the magic of it." He popped a CD into his stereo and a good-time-easy rock 'n' roll melody bounced out of his speakers: "Well, count me in. I'm gonna stand right by your side through thick or thin."

"This can be our theme song!" Marcus shouted to me as Clarence's saxophone thundered in exuberant rips, and we roared over the hills, first to the post office and then on to gussy up a pack of lonely-heart dogs.

Eleven

THE CRAZY-GOOD THING ABOUT DOGS IS if you're nice enough to them, most every single one will get happy— even if it's locked up behind bars. As soon as Marcus put the key into the back-door lock, I could hear them get excited. He walked in and twenty dogs were up, yip-yapping, jumping on the cage doors, their tails wagging, wagging, wagging. He walked down the line of inmates, saying hello, calling each by name: Ace, Butch, Rowdy, Rocky. They were mostly mutts, genetic mishmashes of country dogs used for all types of hunting—foxhounds, Jack Russells, setters, springer spaniels, beagles—and the occasional pit bull or corgi. With such strange mixtures of physical features, none would win a dog show beauty contest. But they sure got adorable with the littlest bit of attention.

"Will these dogs get adopted, Marcus?" I asked.

"That's what we're here to remedy," he answered. "Some of them have been here for weeks, and it's beginning to show in their eyes. Like this one."

He stopped in front of a Labrador retriever, who sat waiting for him, whimper-whining, gazing through the wire mesh with solemn, sad eyes. She was truly pretty. But she had a beard of white around her muzzle, and— there's no other way of saying it—she was downright obese.

"Here's Midnight, the one I was hoping you could take home," he said. "She's the sweetest thing, but nobody wants her because she's old and needs to lose a bunch of weight to ease the strain on her legs. She's had a passel of puppies. I bet she was a good mother; she's so gentle. She was turned in by one of those thousand-dollar-a-puppy pedigree breeders. He said times were bad, and he just couldn't afford her anymore. I'm thinking the jerk didn't want to pay for her old age."

He reached through the bars to scratch her ears. She licked his hand.

"Why don't you take her, Marcus?"

"I wish I could. But we already have my dad's pointer he takes hunting and two dogs I brought home when they'd been here for weeks and weeks with no takers. According to Mom's tarot cards, another stray would make our trailer explode." He winked at me. "Her way of saying she doesn't want another dog."

I laughed.

"All righty, then." He clapped his hands together. "Let's get cracking."

Balancing an armload of brushes, I followed Marcus outside to set up a dog beautician corner. Because our county shelter also rescues mistreated horses, it has several fenced paddocks where the dogs can have a real romp. We let four out at a time to run and tumble all over one another before taking them aside for their beautifying.

For a while, I raced around with them as Marcus tended to his chores. They jumped all over me to get some petting. I even convinced a couple to do dance circles around me. Without bacon! I guess dogs that desperate to please just catch on fast.

Marcus came out to check on me right as I got one of the oddest-looking dogs—sorry, there's just no other word for a mutt that's part bloodhound and part corgi— to twirl following my hand. "Hey, that's pretty cool, Ariel. You should be a dog trainer."

"Thanks!" I grinned and started to tell him about Duke. After all, I'd promised Sergeant Josie I'd ask

Marcus about bringing Duke in to check for a chip. So far, there hadn't been any answers to the Found Dog posts we'd made on local community websites. But Josie said the shelter would have a wand that could detect a microchip if Duke had one. I wished I didn't always keep my promises. What if he did have a chip and I had to give him up? I made myself start to ask Marcus about it—feeling like I was trying to cough up a bowling ball as I did—but was saved by a phone ringing inside.

As Marcus darted to answer, a packet of nicotine chewing gum fell out of his pocket. He must be trying to quit, I thought, with a little spasm of wow-someone-listened-to-me sense of pride! I bent to retrieve it, but a class-clown dog named Spike grabbed the package and dashed around, waving it in front of the other dogs to tease them. They chased him. I chased them. Finally I nabbed Spike to pry the gum out of his teeth. He spat that packet out at me with a full-barrel sneeze. I swear that mutt looked like he was guffawing as I wiped his slobber and snot off my legs.

Getting to work, I brushed their coats to a shine. Those dogs sure loved the attention. They pinwheeled to follow the currycomb on their butts. Others got all greedy and rolled over to get their bellies rubbed, too. The funniest thing was when their back paws started scratching the air in rhythm with the brushstrokes.

The only one who sat absolutely calm was Midnight. I spent extra time getting her sleek coat to glisten. Marcus came out again just as I finished. She'd lain down and crossed one front paw over the other in a ladylike little V.

"I swear that dog is regal as a queen," he said. "Midnight should ride on a float for the parade!"

The Parade.

I looked up at Marcus with that surprise you get when someone says something totally by accident that sets your imagination flying. Suddenly I saw Midnight sitting atop a flowery float following along behind Duke and me dancing, the crowd clapping and cheering. "Hey, Marcus . . . ," I started.

But two cars rolled into the parking lot. "Customers!" Marcus held up crossed fingers before calling all the dogs in to their kennels and going to unlock the front door.

I stayed outside, feeling the need to wander and have a good think on the BIG IDEA that was now rumbling around in my head. The shelter was atop a hill, giving me a long view to the rolling Blue Ridge Mountains painted in that soft spring green of trees budding up in velvety, baby leaves. Splashed here and there were touches of pearl white from dogwoods.

I closed my eyes and listened. A catbird was singing its heart out, mimicking the call of a titmouse, then a cardinal, then a blue jay, then a string of riffs I couldn't identify. He clearly was convinced spring was on its way and was establishing his nesting territory with music. Verse after show-off verse. I felt his song passing over me and opened my eyes to see that bird backlit by the sun, free-form composing and flying at the same time.

Walking down the hill from the paddocks to a creek branch that wiggled its way through the fields and trees, I was met by a sea of one of my favorite things: spring beauties, tiny pinkish wildflowers. I plopped myself down in them and almost rolled like a horse in clover. Honestly, if you have trouble feeling awe, a sense of higher whatever, look into the dime-sized face of a spring beauty. Each white petal is streaked with delicate pink lines that my science teacher would say are meant to lure in pollinating insects. But those pen-and-ink fine stripes don't *need* to be so heart-achingly gorgeous. The fact they are says something astounding, don't you think, about the creativity of life?

Nature's beauty is not always so obvious, of course. Take that deceptively dull-looking, gray catbird. Nothing eye-catching about him. He even lets out a pretty appalling caterwaul when he feels threatened and wants to warn off creatures he doesn't like the looks of. But when he sings—he's sheer poetry. The bird world's star jazz vocalist! You'd completely miss his improvisational magic—his lovely ever-changing medley of melodies— if all you thought about was his appearance.

I don't know why my moods swing so wide so fast sometimes, but that pretty blissful revelation switched abruptly to fill me with frustration. Wasn't I like that catbird? I had thoughts worth hearing. I had creativity aching to sing out. If people took a second to not just look but to listen, they'd recognize that.

Back at my house, my own sister had basically just called me a dog. How could people who should love me make me feel so awful?

Each thought hit me like a gut-punch. I felt sick. Then I got mad, swelling up with fury. I'll show them. I'll show them all, I thought.

As my thoughts whirled around like a tornado, growing wilder by the second, the scent of the flowers and the creek deepened the way they do when shadows spill quickly across the land. I looked up. The tree leaves were contorting in a sudden wind. Cold air slashed my face.

I turned around. A tsunami-big squall line surged

toward me from the mountains. In the distance, heavy curtains of angry rain were pounding the earth and sweeping my way fast. How in the world did that tempest blow up so fast? It was like it had been conjured. I raced for the animal shelter. By the time I reached the back door, I had to really fight to open it against the winds.

Inside, Marcus was finishing up adoption paperwork for a family. I couldn't believe it. They were taking that bad-boy dog, Spike.

"Why not Midnight?" I whispered.

Marcus shook his head. "They thought Spike was more fun."

As the family drove away, the rain hit, pelting and ricocheting off the roof and pavement. Gales battered the windows. And it's the strangest thing—I swear I heard chimes ringing, just like those hanging on Sergeant Josie's porch. I looked out the windows, figuring I'd see a bunch jangling in the wind. I saw nothing but storm water gushing out over the gutters like a thunderous waterfall.

"Hear that, Marcus?"

"Yeah, some storm." He nodded.

"No, those chimes."

He held still a moment, listening. "No, I don't hear any bells. Do your ears hurt? Maybe you're working up an infection. Sometimes that makes my ears ring."

"No, it's . . . it's wind chimes." I heard them plain as day. Was I nuts?

Marcus frowned. "Oh! Wait a minute. I've got a text. That must be what you heard. Good ears!" He checked his phone. "Just Mom, making sure I was okay in the storm." He texted back.

That did it. The fact that Marcus's mother would check on her twenty-year-old son and my parents didn't seem to worry a bit about where I was in hurricane-strong winds split a chasm in my heart. Just as the heavens had kicked open a floodgate to rain, I spewed out my sorrows since we were now officially friends with a theme song and all. I told Marcus how lost I felt at home without George. How that hurt led me to the hills and then to Duke and Sergeant Josie. About dog dancing. How wonderful meshing with the music felt. How awesome—like witnessing a little miracle—it was to see Duke let go of his fear as he danced with me.

I even confessed my idea of crashing the parade. My hope that—if people saw what I could imagine and create—they would stop thinking I was some kind of failure in the making. The only thing I didn't share was the spiteful part about wanting to steal the show from G-L-O-R-I-A.

"Shoot, Ariel. That rocks."

"Really?"

"Heck yeah!"

"I was thinking, Marcus. After you said she was as regal as an Apple Blossom queen. Maybe I should take Midnight, too. If I put her in the parade and get her to dance even just a little, someone's sure to want to take her home. Don't you think?"

Marcus grinned. "There, you see? Being smart *is* good. I never would have come up with that." He stuck out his lower lip in thought. "The poor old girl is in danger of being euthanized soon if we can't find her a home."

I gasped.

He nodded, thoughtful. "I'll sign her out as if I'm adopting her so you can take her. Have you got a place to keep her?"

I pondered a moment. I couldn't ask Sergeant Josie to take another dog. "Oh! Wait! Our barn has stall doors that still close. I might could hide her there."

Then another idea hit me. An even bigger, better idea. "Marcus, you know what would be really great? I could take some of the other girl dogs, too, and they could be princesses to Midnight. Wouldn't that be fun? I could spruce them up and maybe get them to do a little something to the music, too."

I could be like George leading a whole marching band through the streets during the parade. I'd wow everybody!

"Now hold on, Ariel, that's getting a little crazy, don't you think?" Marcus said. "How are you going to handle that many dogs? Besides, I don't know, making a dog court like the princesses' seems kind of disrespectful. A lot of folks around here, including me, are really proud of that parade. Shoot, it's been going on near a hundred years. There's nothing else like it, anywhere. We've got all those celebrities that come to be grand marshal. And . . . and . . . I don't think Gloria would like that at all."

"I'm not being disrespectful of *the parade*, Marcus. I love it, too. But this idea is epic, don't you see? Ironic! It'll prove even 'real dogs,'"—I made air quotes—"can be beautiful in their own way. We can prove that beauty is really about dreams. Creativity. Hard work. Originality. Heart. It'll be . . ." There were those chimes again.

Marcus patted his pocket and pulled his phone out. "Ah." He smiled. "It's from Glorious Gloria. Speak of the devil."

That's about right, I thought.

Marcus walked away from me to open the text in private. As he read, his typically sunny face turned stony.

His expression scared the bejeebees out of me. What if Gloria had some horrible news about George? I tried to never think about the reality that George could get hurt or . . . "What's wrong?" I asked.

Marcus ignored me. Striding to the window to get better reception—because now thunder and lightning were rocking the shelter—Marcus thumbed in a number and put the phone to his ear. He redialed six times before my sister picked up.

"What's going on, Gloria?" Marcus's voice sounded like his eyes had looked when he caught me being such a snob about him.

He listened for a long time before saying, "Speak the truth and blind the devil, girl. Did your mother put you up to this?"

Plugging one ear with a finger against the raging storm, he listened. Then he held the phone out to look at it. The call had dropped. Or Gloria had hung up on him. He called back, letting it ring and ring. No answer. Called again. Nothing.

Marcus put his forehead against the windowpane. His shoulders started shaking. The rain fell, and Marcus sobbed, tears against tears through glass.

I knew the call wasn't about George. I pretty much figured what it was about, but finally I asked, "Are you okay, Marcus? What happened?"

Slowly, Marcus stopped crying. He stared out the window, wiped his face with his sleeve, and handed me his cell phone without turning around.

The message read: *I can't see you anymore. I'm sorry.*

"Oh, Marcus," I murmured in sympathy. Leave it to G-L-O-R-I-A to dump a boyfriend via text. I had suspected she'd break up with him once she got up on her high throne of the float. I guessed her being fitted that morning for the pink ball gown she'd wear in the parade convinced her of Mama's argument that Marcus no longer fit her life. Typical. But doing it by text? I was furious for him. And ashamed for her. She needed to be taught a lesson—bad, I fumed. She needed to feel what it felt like to be thrown away as junk.

Lightning lit up the room, thunder *kabanged*, and the lights went out. When the generator kicked up and emergency floodlights snapped on, Marcus was staring at me, the strangest look in his eyes as he asked: "How many dogs did you say you wanted?"

In pouring rain, thunderclaps, and lightning explosions, we crammed Midnight and five other girl dogs into the back of Marcus's Mustang. It's like they knew they were making a prison break: they were so quiet and cooperative, even as all the boy dogs we were leaving behind howled and scratched at their doors. I felt so sorry for the ones we couldn't take—they were so upset, baying and jumping and crying—I tossed fistfuls of dog biscuits into their cages. If I could have, I would have sprung every last one of them.

Only as we drove off did I dare talk to Marcus again; he'd been so angry-silent. He hadn't locked the back door. I worried that he should.

Marcus's voice was cold as he answered, "I left it open on purpose. It'll look like I made a stupid mistake and that the dogs got out or someone came in and stole them."

"But Marcus, no one will ever think you were that careless." I'd seen how gentle he was with those dogs, how clean he made the shelter kennels, how methodical he was filling out paperwork for adoptions.

"Sure they will." His eyes narrowed. "They'll figure that I am just some dumb hillbilly."

"But Marcus, you'll get in a lot of trouble."

Only then did he soften a bit. "Ariel, you really can be a good friend. I won't forget that. But I'm leaving tomorrow. No need to stick around now. Leaving that door open is like burning a bridge so I can't chicken out. No turning back. Carpe diem."

"Oh, Marcus, where will you go?"

He was quiet for a moment before carefully reciting, "'The wind blows where it wishes and you hear the sound of it, but cannot tell where it comes from or where it goes.'"

"Where did you read that?" I asked.

"The Book of John."

"What does it mean?"

"I'm no theologian," Marcus answered, "but I take that passage to mean everything will be all right even though I don't know my direction yet. As long as I have faith and hope and follow what my heart tells me is right. No matter how much hurt's been done me.

"That'll do fine," he muttered. "I'll go wherever these storm winds blow me."

Before he drove off into the tempest, Marcus did me one last solid, as he'd say. He helped me sneak the girls into our barn and bed them down together in a big stall. They followed him in that storm as trustingly as puppies trot along behind their mother. I did, too. Once inside, the girls curled up in one slobbery heap of happy as we filled buckets with water for them. To keep from giving ourselves away, we did it all in silence and by the small beam thrown by a flashlight Marcus kept in his glove compartment.

As he closed the rusty bolt on the stall door, Marcus asked, "Will you be okay from here?"

I nodded. I felt a big lump in my throat.

He reached out and ruffled my hair. "See ya, Ariel." Then he turned and seeped into the shadows of the night.

But before he disappeared entirely, I ran to catch up and threw my arms around his waist from behind. "Thank you, Marcus. I think you're even better than any Roman emperor."

Then I stepped back and he was gone. With the thunder and winds wailing I couldn't hear his car start or the sound of his tires on our lane. I just felt him set sail.

I wish I could tell you that Marcus's forgiveness or zen or sense of destiny blew into my soul and washed away my fury. But it didn't. My winds were shoving me in a totally different direction. And I felt the strangest excitement knowing I finally had a battle plan—no matter how storm-child weird it might seem.

Twelve

AT FIVE THIRTY THE NEXT MORNING, my alarm clock jarred me awake. I dressed fast and slipped out of the house in the early-morning dimness to head for the barn. I'd heard the dogs howling during the night as the storm raged on for hours, like it had parked itself right over my bedroom. Somehow everyone else seemed to have slept through the cacophony, figuring their baying to be the wind, I guessed. But if the dogs started barking again this morning, someone would go investigating, for sure.

In the growing pink dawn light, what had seemed a brilliant idea the day before was looking like one of the stupidest ever. Marcus had given me a huge bag of kibble so I could keep them fed. But how was I going to keep the girls quiet? How was I going to explain six dogs to my family if they were found?

I picked my way over branches the storm had ripped

off and flung around like a mad game of pick-up-sticks. The soggy ground sucked at my shoes. Rainwater was still beaded in crystals along trees and dripped in soft cadence from the leaves. A Carolina wren called, "Wheat-eater, wheat-eater, wheat," and then darted from tree to tree in front of me—like he was leading me someplace.

There was something Narnia mystical about that morning. Fog hazed everything. So thick, I didn't even notice the red fox sitting by the barn door until I was almost on top of it. It waited until I could have reached out and touched it before taking off at a gallop in a flash of red.

"Yeah, you better run," I muttered. "If these dogs got out, that'd be the end of you." And me. Even the quietest dogs have a fit when they smell fox. You should hear the yelping of the local hunt's hounds when they catch a whiff of their quarry.

I was a little surprised the fox had been there to begin with. Not that it was unusual for one of them to be sniffing for field mice around our barn, but normally the smell of dogs would have scared it off fast. I glanced back at the fox to make sure it wasn't rabid or something. Everyone around here knows to call animal control quick at the sight of a fox with a mangy thin tail.

The fox ran along our driveway. I tracked him but

couldn't see well in the gloom until it reached where our lane meets the road. There, one lonely lamppost shines into the darkness so people can find our place at night. No, the fox's tail was a beautiful, full plume of fiery red as long as its body. He took one last look at me before hopping over an embankment and disappearing. Watching him, I noticed something else red. I squinted into the mist. A cherry-red pickup was parked by the side of the road.

It was like the fox was trying to warn me! For a second I went weak with panic. Was it the sheriff? Setting up a speed trap for weekend joy-riders? He'd hear the dogs. Oh my God, Oh my God, Oh my God.

Wait. I made myself slow down my brain and think.

No self-respecting sheriff would give himself away with a bright red truck. It was someone else's. Strange that it was just sitting there by the side of the road. Was someone snooping around the barn? In a dither of worry, I threw my weight on the heavy barn door to slide it open, not exactly knowing what I'd do if someone was inside—bean them with one of the old pitchforks hanging on the wall?

I almost fell over at the sight.

There sat Sergeant Josie, surrounded by all six dogs, facing her like kindergartners listening to a librarian at story-time. They didn't budge as I came in, even with the booming grate of that door as I pushed it. It was like she had them under some kind of spell. Or maybe it was they who had her.

"What are you doing?" I felt the need to whisper; the morning and the scene before me felt that enchanted. I tiptoed closer, and only then did the dogs turn their heads to pant happily in my direction.

"I was worried when you didn't come to the cabin yesterday since it was Saturday and no school," said Sergeant Josie. "The cabin has old phone books. I looked up your house number and was going to call. But I wondered if that would get you in trouble somehow. It also listed your address, so . . ." She trailed off. "Everything okay?"

She'd wondered where I was! I kind of teared up but then just nodded in reply, looking cool, I hoped. I didn't want to freak her out, thinking that now she needed to adopt me or something. "Where's Duke?"

"I couldn't get him out of the truck. I swear he's standing post." Sergeant Josie smiled. "I wouldn't have gotten out myself—I was just kind of driving by to make sure . . ." She shrugged. "Anyway, I wouldn't have gotten out except I heard barking."

One of the dogs woofed at her happily, once, like it had

been cued to say, "That's right."

She laughed.

Another yip-yapped and then silenced.

Sergeant Josie laughed again. I'd never seen her that at ease. "I swear they invited me in," she said. "We've been sitting like this for quite a while. Did you train them to do this?"

I shook my head. "I've only had them overnight."

Sergeant Josie grew serious. "Really? You know, I keep a police radio scanner in the truck. As I was driving here, I heard chatter about a break-in at the animal shelter. All the female dogs are missing. Six of them."

She made a point of counting out loud: "One-two-three-four-five-six." She crossed her arms and fixed me with an emphatic is-there-something-you-want-to-tell-me look. "The police are thinking it was a robbery. They were checking to make sure no dangerous meds were taken."

The police already knew! And they were thinking it could be a real heist? Oh no. Had I gotten Marcus in serious trouble?

"It's not like that at all, Sergeant, I swear!" I scrambled to explain in a torrent of words: "I went there to help beautify these dogs to help get them adopted. I went with Marcus, Gloria's boyfriend—well, he was, but she dumped him by text, because he's what she would call a hick and she's a princess, and . . . and . . . and I was real upset. And he was all upset. And I thought maybe these dogs could be Duke's princesses in the parade, and that that would be really funny, and maybe . . . maybe people would love them if they saw them dance, too, and adopt them. And then he told me that was a good idea because they might be put to sleep on account of no one wanting them, on account of their not being pretty enough, and I don't think dogs should be ignored or thrown away or eutha-eutha-eutha-what's-it because people who are supposed to love them don't like them or find them annoying or clumsy or embarrassing or not picture perfect and well . . . well, so we decided to spring them from their cages. And . . . and . . . and you can just arrest me, sir, ma'am. It's my fault. It was my idea, not Marcus's. Don't do anything bad to Marcus, Marcus was just being nice to me, Marcus didn't do anything stupid except love my sister."

With that I ran out of breath.

Sergeant Josie listened all the way through. For a horrifying moment, she said nothing. Then she asked solemnly, "Marcus is a friend of yours?"

I nodded.

"You know what I've learned may be the most

important thing in the world?"

Shaking my head, my heart sinking, I figured she was going to tell me that it was following rules. The rules of law, as Daddy would say.

"Sticking by your buddies." Sergeant Josie looked around the circle of dogs. "And being kind to those who need help."

I gasped, too relieved to speak.

She smiled reassuringly at me. "What are their names?"

I realized I had no idea; Marcus and I had been so hurried. "That one's Midnight. But I don't know the others."

"Midnight?" She bent and kissed Midnight's head. "The time the world shifts into a new day, with new possibilities and hope. Although it's too dark to look very far into the future." She smiled. "Seems appropriate."

I stared at the top of Sergeant Josie's head as she hugged the Labrador. She must have gotten to a poetry collection or something on her reading syllabus. "Who said that?" I asked.

"Just me," she murmured. She stood and paced, finally stopping to lean against the barn door. She considered me for a long minute. I held my breath. When people stand right by a door, I always worry they might walk out on me if I give the wrong answer.

Finally, Midnight broke the stare between us. She heaved herself up, waddled over, and cozied up right next to Sergeant Josie. Resting her muzzle on Sergeant Josie's leg, Midnight gazed up earnestly at her. *Thump, thump, thump* went her tail.

"Wow." Sergeant Josie's voice choked a little as she whispered to Midnight, "Your expression is just like my dog when . . ." She cleared her throat. She looked over at me. "You know, Ariel, one of the things about that cabin of mine—no one other than you and Duke have found their way to it." She waited for me to get what that info implied.

"Oh, Sergeant Josie!" At that I did burst into tears—grateful and touched and embarrassed and unsure all at the same time. "Do you think you could hide them for a while?"

"For the time being. I like your idea about trying to find them new owners at the parade. Like one of those adopt-a-pet days at farmers' markets and Petcos. We'll have to check the people out, of course. But we can figure that out later." She straightened up. "What should we call them?"

Their names came easy to me, dog heroes from books I'd loved. I didn't worry about gender: Duchess and Kep from Beatrix Potter's picture books, Bodger from *The Incredible Journey*, Jump from Tamora Pierce's series, and, of course, Lassie.

Right then, lights snapped on in the kitchen across the lawn. One of the few things Mama did consistently (other than bragging on G-L-O-R-I-A) was go to church most Sundays. Sometimes she even went as early as the eight o'clock service if she had things she had to do later in the day like shopping. That would be her, making French Vanilla Cinnamon coffee, about the only thing she started from scratch.

"Time to move out," whispered Sergeant Josie. "Let's get these ladies into my truck."

In single silent file, following right behind her, those dogs marched themselves straight to Sergeant Josie's truck—no wandering off following their noses, no jockeying to get ahead of one another. Duke was sitting in the truck bed. When he spotted me, he dove out right into my arms.

I love that dog.

So did Midnight, Duchess, Kep, Bodger, Jump, and Lassie! They happily let him escort them to the truck. We had to lift Midnight into the pickup's bed, which was no easy task, but the rest of the girls easily jumped in. They lay down quiet as could be so when Sergeant Josie and I closed the end gate, the dogs weren't even visible. And when she drove off, not one poked her head up like most mutts do, snuffing the wind, their ears and tongues flapping. It was as if they knew they were on a mission!

I watched the truck disappear round the bend before turning back for the house.

When I darted into the kitchen, I discovered Mama staring into her coffee, trying to wake herself up. I held my breath, but all she said was that she was in the mood for all of us to go to church together to petition God for G-L-O-R-I-A's success. She ordered me upstairs to wake everyone. No questions about what I had been doing outside that early—a non-reaction I should have expected and not been all worried about her noticing six dogs trooping into a bright red truck at the end of our lane. There didn't seem to be enough coffee in the world to make her concerned about my whereabouts.

The scene when we arrived at church, on the other hand, was exactly what I expected. Gloria had slept in the past few Sundays, so her adoring fans were thrilled to see her. "Oh, Glooooori-aaaa!" the church ladies chorused as we approached the vestibule doorway. They crushed her in excited, fluttering hugs, wreathed in sweet perfumes, and chattered all at once. "I'm so proud of you." "Isn't it marvelous?" "You'll be the belle of the parade." "This is the beginning of great things." "I'll be able to tell reporters writing your life story that I knew you when you were just a little girl."

Then they swooped onto Mama, congratulating her for raising such a beauty. "Of course, she looks just like you." "You two are the Gilmore Girls, I swear." "Hollywood could cast you two in a mother-daughter movie."

They swarmed Daddy. "Your jacket must be bursting its buttons, mister." "Aren't you proud beyond anything?" "What a lucky man to be surrounded by *two* such beautiful women each and every day."

Me? "Good morning, Ariel."

The flock scattered into pews.

During the service, the minister urged us to not let the vanities of this earth corrupt our God-given goodness. I'm sorry to report—since I was sitting there in church and should have been having peaceful, righteous thoughts—that I did hope G-L-O-R-I-A was feeling sick to her soul with guilt about how mean she'd been to Marcus. The only real prayer I squeezed out of myself, other than my usual plea about keeping George safe, was one asking for good winds for Marcus. Oh, and one other about not getting arrested as a dog-snatcher.

I finally managed to tamp down my swirl of angst—so God wouldn't feel the need to smite me right there for thinking such mean thoughts in His house—by contemplating how I was going to dress my princesses for the parade. As the preacher tried hard to save my sorry soul, I imagined Gloria's closet and rummaged her drawers in my mind's eye—smiling the whole time. Yup, there would be some fine outfits there for me to borrow for my dog court.

Thirteen

FOR THE NEXT TWO WEEKS, GLORIA and Mama were consumed with beautifying everything about G-L-O-R-I-A, like polishing up an apple before handing it to a teacher. She had her hair highlighted, her nails buffed, painted, and sealed with gel, her legs waxed. She even went to a tanning salon—which I tried warning her off from, because even as mad as I was at her, I didn't want her to get skin cancer. But Mama hushed me, saying Gloria needed to be bronzed and I needed to stop being such a killjoy.

Normally, all that fuss and bother about G-L-O-R-I-A might have upset me. But I was focusing on my own preparations, climbing the blooming hills to heaven: music, dance, and a dog who came alive with happiness when he saw me.

Every day Duke and I practiced, chiseling away

clumsiness and hesitation. Since we no longer needed to count out rhythms, our dance routine was becoming second nature, poetry-in-motion. The song had seeped into our souls and become our heartbeat. We were in complete sync with the melody and each other.

Duke seemed so much more relaxed. He even followed me in and out of the cabin door with only a flinch here and there. And truth be told, I was more at peace, too. When I was with Sergeant Josie, I didn't feel quite so abandoned. Her being a veteran and all made me feel closer to George.

I'd never been one for dress-up or playing with dolls, but I sure was having fun planning the costumes for the parade. Up in the attic, I'd found an old top hat, the kind that folds down and then pops up like a little chimney stack when you snap it against your hand. It was way cool. On it, Sergeant Josie superglued a chin strap to secure it to Duke's head during our dance. I'd also found a white vest and bowtie men wear with formal dinner jackets. Duke was going to look all *Great Gatsby* in it, Sergeant Josie said. I guess she'd just gotten to Fitzgerald on her reading list.

In the same cedar closet I discovered dresses from the 1940s, when Duke Ellington—the big-band musician Stevie Wonder celebrated in his song—was big. Rummaging through them, I pulled out a gorgeous velvet dress with beaded shoulders, made of a rich emerald, the color of a bower in the woods thick with summer-full leaves. When I held it against me in front of the mirror of an old vanity abandoned under the eaves, its beads glimmered. The color made my dull hazel eyes suddenly look interesting cat-eye-green. Astonished, right there and then in the attic's dust I stripped to my underwear and winnowed into that evening gown's soft folds. It fit!

Whoever wore that dress before was as tall and lean, and maybe even as gangly, as I am. I wondered if it had been Daddy's mother. I'd stared enough at her photo that I could definitely see some resemblance in our profiles—the same long face and nose. I decided to believe it was my grandmother's dress. Her being such a big reader, and making such smart comments about books, made me think having some of my grandmother's genes floating around in me might not be so bad. I could wear that dress with a sense of family tradition and pride I rarely felt.

I twirled. It swirled—like a dancer. It was absolutely perfect.

For my pooch escapees, I raided Gloria's overflowing wardrobe and collected an armful of things in the traditional Blossom Festival colors of pink and green—crisp cotton boyfriend shirts with pop-up collars, sweaters embroidered with flowers. In the back of her closet was the Sugar Plum Fairy tutu Daddy had mistakenly remembered me wearing. That would be for Midnight. As I tiptoed out of her bedroom, I was tempted to make off with Gloria's teen-queen tiara that rested on top of her bureau mirror. But even I wasn't that reckless. There were plenty of hair bows and headbands. The girls were going to look sweet.

Not that everything was perfect. According to the local newspaper, police were still asking questions about what reporters dubbed "the dog-pound prison break." But beyond that, not much investigating was going on. Let's face it, my escapees weren't exactly prized pets, so no one was offering rewards or taping pictures on stop signs.

No, my main problem was that my jailbird dogs were a straight-up disaster, dance-wise. Duke and I couldn't do our routine over and over for the whole parade—it snaked through Winchester for twenty-plus blocks. We needed to alternate with the girls. Mostly they could just sit like princesses on Sergeant Josie's truck while Duke and I walked ahead of them. But they had to do a little *something* now and then. Even a princess like Gloria waved and smiled at the street crowds.

Sergeant Josie and I decorated her truck with plastic flowers and put crates in the bed for the girls to perch on during the parade. But getting them to sit still and stay was beginning to feel like *Mission: Impossible.* As grateful as those dogs were to be sprung from their cages and as hard as they tried to please, they got way too distracted, way too easily. Every chipmunk, every salamander, every bird, every deer—geez, even every pine cone that fell to the ground with a soft thump caused a conga-line commotion. One would start barking and leap off the porch, and the rest followed, racing off to nab whatever it was that caught the first dog's attention.

Seeing how they followed one another, I tried setting up a line dance for them, like the electric slide. Big mistake! All those wagging tails caused total havoc. The girls couldn't stop friendly chewing on each other when the dog in front turned and accidentally swatted the one behind her in the face.

I tried to get them to bob their heads from side to side in unison. But that just seemed to remind them they needed a good scratch. And when one did, they all did, in a growing crescendo of *scritch . . . scritch . . . scritch . . . scr-scr-scr-scr-scri-scriiiiiiitch. BARK!* It was like George's marching band percussion section doing a slow-grow drumroll ending in a cymbal crash.

I taught them to circle, but they thought it was so much fun, they couldn't stop. They'd go round and round, bumping each other into piles of flailing, yapping dogs. When I finally calmed them down enough to sit, they were all too twitchy to *really* listen.

If I paid attention to one, the others rushed to scratch at my knees in a doggie look-at-me free-for-all. Jump was the worst. She was living up to her name and must have had some border collie in her—you know, those fluffy dogs that can hurl themselves six feet into the air to catch a Frisbee—because she kept leaping over the others to slurp my face, all four paws suspended in the air. She knocked me to the ground every time.

Honestly, only Sergeant Josie had any control over them. She would hold up her pointer finger, then two fingers, then three, the way kindergarten teachers count down seconds for children to settle into their seats and— *shazam*—all those dogs got quiet. It helped, of course, that she rewarded them with bacon. But when I took over, chaos reigned.

Except with Midnight. She was always dignified and attentive. It would have been easy to set the entire choreography on her because she *listened.* But the truth was the old girl was too arthritic to get up and rhumba.

One afternoon, when all the dogs went scattering,

barking at each other, I flung myself down beside Sergeant Josie. She'd been watching from the porch, reading again. Duke flopped beside me, blowing out a huge snuffy sigh all over me. He'd had it with the girls, too. "This is not working." I whined.

Sergeant Josie simply turned a page.

I repeated my complaint.

"I heard you, Ariel." She turned another page with crisp emphasis.

I sat up. Why wasn't she helping? I frowned. "What are you reading that's so all-fired interesting?" I wasn't afraid of her anymore, obviously.

"It isn't so much interesting"—Sergeant Josie looked up at me—"as . . . disturbing. Beautifully written. But its world is hitting me a little hard."

"What is it?"

She held it up so I could read the cover: *The Kite Runner*. I noticed her hands were shaking. I hadn't seen that for a while. "What's it about?"

"Two boys who fly kites in a tournament." She sighed. "Cruelty. Love. Redemption. Racism." She looked out the window. "It's set in Afghanistan."

"Oh." I hesitated. "Should I read it? So I know more about what George is seeing over there?"

My question pulled Josie's gaze back to me. She

studied me for a moment. "Not yet. When he gets back."

I was grateful for her using the word *when*.

A breeze picked up and backhanded the porch bells into little tinkles. Their jangles set off Lassie into a soulful barking. Jump, Duchess, Bodger, and Kep chimed in.

Sergeant Josie laughed at them and shut her novel. "I can tell you're looking for answers from me, Ariel. But the job of a good trainer, or friend for that matter, is not to tell you exactly what to do but to be more of a compass to help you get your bearings. That way you map your own journey. You find your own definition, not one put on you by other people's opinions. Do you understand?"

I just wanted some help with the dogs. How hard was that? But Sergeant Josie had hit on something I definitely felt—I was tired of being defined by others. So I muttered, "I suppose."

She smiled. "Okay, look. This is what I see. Each of those dogs has her own rhythm." She pointed to the cascade of bells hanging from her porch roof. "Kind of like how each of my wind chimes has its own pitch. The wind brushes them to nudge each to sing out with its own note. Then each solitary tone harmonizes with the rest of the group, making chords of melody, a rich, collective, and cooperative song, a communion among individual souls."

Sergeant Josie waited for that to sink in. Dang, that woman sure could be all poetical when she put her mind to it. I got her metaphor. Or was it a simile? I get those two confused sometimes.

Seeing me thinking, Sergeant Josie nodded toward the clearing where the girls had bolted. Jump was leaping and rolling around like an Olympic gymnast dancing a floor exercise. Lassie pirouetted as she chased her own tail. When she caught it, she backed away still clamped down on it, like she was exiting, stage left. Bodger was circling all of them in perfect serpentines. Duchess was looking up to the sky, cross-stepping as she tracked squirrels jumping across branches. Kep stood on her hind legs like a ballerina *en pointe*, gracefully rounding the tree that the squirrels had raced up to safety. And Midnight? Well, Midnight sat elegantly, just watching, even as a squirrel nearly darted over her feet in its panic to elude Duchess.

I watched for a few minutes, trying to spot a choreography that could include all their individual moves. When Daddy compared me to Martha Graham, I hadn't been sure if it was a compliment or not. So I'd looked her up. It actually may have been one of the nicest things Daddy's ever said to me. Martha Graham is called the mother of modern dance. She rejected classical ballet's rigid froufrou and fairy-princess stereotypes of prettiness and instead had the imagination and courage to let her dancers be more real, more athletic, more out there emotion-wise. Martha Graham would probably tell me Sergeant Josie was right. These girls weren't suited to coordinated lock-step ballet.

George's feelings about what made music so powerful came back to me: "It's ripping yourself open, A, and letting the world watch your heart ache with each beat."

Of course. The girls just needed to jam. For me to give them the freedom to be themselves and to express what they felt without worrying what they looked like when they were doing it. That would bring out the natural beauty in them.

Suddenly I knew exactly what song to play for them!

Fourteen

ON THE MORNING OF THE GRAND parade, in 5 a.m. darkness, I heard an engine *rev-revving* outside our lane. Sergeant Josie's signal. She'd loaded our beauties into her truck and come to pick me up with reconnaissance stealth. No headlight beams, just that surge of engine. *Vroom, vroom.* A windblast of horsepower at a starting gate. *Vroom, vroom.* Time to go. *Vroom, vroom.* No turning back now.

Dashing across the yard, I clutched a pillowcase bulging with costumes for my pooches. My grandmother's emerald dress slapped my legs as I ran.

The whole morning would need clandestine cunning, starting with getting us on the road and away from the house without anyone noticing. Then we'd need to sneak into the parade lineup of bands, clowns, antique cars, and floats—participants who had registered and been approved months before. That was the only plan I'd been able to come up with: getting situated among the parade vehicles before anyone was really awake and then acting totally chill like we belonged. You see it in adventure movies all the time, right? Just blend in with the crowd.

Sergeant Josie thought that strategy was pretty flimsy. But she went along with it, not seeing any other option this late in the parade game. "Another important thing I learned in Afghanistan," she'd warned, "is that no matter how much planning goes into a mission, there are sure to be land mines and ambushes. You just gotta be on your toes, keep a sharp eye out for them, and then have the smarts and guts to react. Fast. You can't freeze." She'd paused and added in a whisper, "Then you're dead."

She worried me sometimes. In moments like that, it was obvious that the brooding, sad something that had followed Sergeant Josie home from Afghanistan was still chasing her.

When I reached the truck's back side, my dog queen and her princesses popped their heads up over the cab's gate. But they only happy-whimpered their greeting, no so-glad-to-see-you-I-can't-help-myself barking—thank goodness. I scrambled into the truck's cab, yanking my flapper dress up to my waist to climb in. It's just a truth that I am capable of only so much ladylike grace.

"Look at you! As glamorous as Ginger Rogers."

I beamed. Precisely what I was hoping for—to remind my audience a little sorta kinda of the movie-star dancer who was Fred Astaire's favorite partner. After all, we'd dressed Duke in a top hat, bow tie, and white dinner vest like Astaire wore so often in their ten movies together.

"You know what they say about Ginger, don't you?" asked Sergeant Josie.

I sure did. Together we recited: "She did everything Fred did, backwards and in high heels!"

We laughed.

"Okay, soldier, let's do this thing." Sergeant Josie started driving, slowly, not clicking on her headlights until we were safely away from view of my house.

"Look out!" I shrieked.

Sergeant Josie swerved, barely missing a bunch of deer, which at that very moment decided they just had to jump from an embankment into the road. She managed to avoid them only to come head to head with the next flash mob of leaping does.

She slammed on the brakes. The truck swerved and lurched. Thankfully she'd only been plodding along. Still, all our princesses and Midnight slid into a scrambling, howling jumble against the back window. They let fly in a cacophony of yelps.

"Shhhh! Oh, shhhh!" I begged, pushing open the window to the truck bed so they'd hear me. Those dogs were going to wake up the entire Blue Ridge with their carrying-on.

Tumbling about trying to right themselves, the girls nipped and sniped and yipped at each other. I don't think they could even hear me fussing at them to stop over the noise they were making. Only Duke settled them down, after sticking his head through the window to touch noses with each of those crying canines.

The deer ambled away, flipping their white tails at us.

I was so furious at them for almost seriously hurting my girls, I spluttered, "Can you show me how to shoot that gun of yours so I can eliminate these stupid big rodents!"

Sergeant Josie shook her head. "You don't mean that, Ariel. Besides, I got rid of it."

"Why?" I was shocked. No one around here gets rid of guns. There are people who go out hunting each season in family ritual, using rifles their granddaddies did.

"Because I scared a kid with it," she said, pulling back out into the road.

After that, we drove for a long while in silence. Both of us thinking.

We were counting on the town being groggy from the Festival's string of parties so we could slip in unnoticed. The sheer number of bodies that would crowd the streets that day should shield us as well. During the Festival, the little city of Winchester swells from twenty-seven thousand residents to a quarter of a million visitors.

When it started back in the 1920s to celebrate the Valley's apple industry, the Festival was just a one-day pageant and a parade. It was such a success, the crowning of the queen morphed over the next decade into an extravaganza held on the hillside marble stairs of the city's grand old high school. Dozens of girls in gauzy gowns performed "the step dance," moving in rows of geometric patterns on the wide white stairway. Some years, the fronts of their dresses were pink and the backs green to create waves of colors as they turned. Boy pages dressed in satin and carried the queen's train. Flower girls threw petals for her to walk on. Children clutching blossom branches formed a giant apple tree. I wish I'd seen all that.

Nowadays, the crowning ceremony is held inside, in the high school's Patsy Cline auditorium. It's still full of tradition and processionals, but it's not as elegant or enchanting as those synchronized kaleidoscope routines. Even so, the Festival—or "the Bloom," as locals call it—

has grown into a kind of Virginia Mardi Gras. Lasting a whole week, it has something for everyone—which is part of what I like so much about it.

At a "pumps and pearls" party, women wear pink and green feather boas and create the craziest shoes you've ever seen for a competition. People can do-si-do at a square dance, waltz at "the Young at Heart" party, or get down at a rock 'n' roll blast. The princesses and beauty queens celebrate at fancy-dress balls. Adults run a 10K and kids a "bloomin' mile" course. There's a bluegrass festival, jazz band competition, a prayer brunch, a fire truck rodeo, and an apple pie bake-off.

Come to think of it, individuality is the rule of the Festival. As long as you wear pink or green and like apples, pretty much anything goes. Maybe we'd fit in just fine.

We entered the edges of Old Town.

Even at that early hour, the sidewalks in front of those stately old houses were crammed with green folding chairs and Porta Potties. Floats, fire trucks, and convertibles sat parked bumper to bumper. We avoided the princess floats, knowing there would be too many bystanders taking pictures and stage mothers applying lipstick and blush—including Mama. She and Gloria were due to arrive around eight to check in.

Instead, we slipped ourselves into the lineup of the old farm tractors. They were decorated with flags, plastic flowers, and cutesy country signs with Ns written backward and "git" for "get." The kind of displays that make city people say, "Oh, look, how quaint," as they sip their double-whatever lattes and snap selfies like they would in front of a Smithsonian exhibit.

"There." Sergeant Josie turned off the truck ignition. She pulled in a deep long breath and exhaled, slow. Her hands were shaking. Suddenly she looked terrible.

"Are you okay?" My first thought, of course, was selfish. She wasn't going to get sick on me, was she? I couldn't do this without her!

"This is the first time in a while that I've been out of the cabin other than to get groceries," she answered. "I've been holed up getting my head straight. Time for reentry, as my VA shrink calls it. Desensitization training."

"What?"

"Exposing myself to negative stimuli to make me stop reacting to it."

"What?"

"Marching back into the windstorm."

"What?"

She snort-laughed, and finally said something I could

understand easily, "Getting back up on the horse that threw you." She gripped the steering wheel tighter. "For me, back here in the States, that 'horse' seems to be big milling crowds of people carrying packages that I can't see the insides of—things my dog and I might have found IEDs in during market days in Afghanistan. That and sudden, loud noises resembling gunfire or small explosives just throw me back. Like that thunderstorm the night we met." She looked over at me. "You're supposed to do exposure therapy in little doses, building up to bigger ones, to develop tolerance to the situation. Unfortunately, there weren't exactly a string of little parades I could practice on."

I gasped. After she told me she had PTSD I'd looked up symptoms on the internet, so I'd know what I was dealing with. So I understood—sort of—why a young, fit-looking army vet would have sequestered herself in an isolated cabin to pull herself back together. But I hadn't realized that someone who had survived terrible battles would be skittish in a plain old American crowd. No wonder she'd felt such empathy for Duke. Suddenly I realized what courage it was taking for Sergeant Josie to have my back at the parade.

I launched myself at her before I could get shy about it and hugged her. "Thank you soooooooo much for coming,

Sergeant Josie. Thank you for . . . for . . . everything."

I didn't let go.

Duke squirmed his way into the embrace to lick her face. Long enough for her stand-at-attention-straight posture to soften and relax and then her hand to reach up to pat my arm. Long enough for her to say, "To be honest, Ariel, I should thank you. You are like that wind-creature in *The Tempest.* You showed up in a storm offering something that helped me deal with the cyclone in my heart. And you brought in old Duke here." She scratched his ear.

"You see, my partner, my dog . . ." She pulled in a deep breath before continuing, "Died in an IED trap." I could feel her swallowing hard. "We'd been out for hours. He'd found dozens of buried bombs along the road. He was already exhausted. Civilians were starting to gather on rooftops to shout curses at us. Any one of them could have been a sniper. The guys wanted to get back to the safety of camp and were getting really antsy because night was coming. I think he sensed their growing anxiety and starting rushing his detection sweep. Then the winds kicked up, blowing sand everywhere, which can mute scents and confuse sniffer dogs. He just didn't smell the last one that . . ." I could barely hear what she whispered next. "It should have been me . . . not him. I should have pulled him out before . . ." She trailed off.

After a long moment she went on, "Anyway, helping you help Duke helped me." She shrugged again, with that crooked, self-conscious smile of hers. "Sounds like the beginning of a country-western song." She kissed me quickly and awkwardly on my head and pulled away. "Go get your princesses ready. I need to find some coffee and take a little walk to clear my head and settle my nerves."

Fifteen

ALREADY DRESSED IN MY GREEN VELVET, I had some trouble swinging myself up into the truck bed. Amazingly, those rambunctious dogs didn't jump all over me as I did. They seemed to know it was showtime. For once, they sat quietly, waiting for me to primp them.

I started with Midnight, who needed help bad. Her pink tutu was up around her neck and splayed out stiff like those huge plastic cones veterinarians put on dogs after surgery to keep them from biting at their stitches. I smoothed it down, tied it around her stomach, and brushed her coat. Then I put on her head the gauzy ballet crown that matched the tutu. She climbed up onto her throne—a bench Sergeant Josie and I had wrapped in pink and green crepe paper—and sat down in a pouf of pink.

One by one I buttoned up the girls' flowery sweaters, tied ribbons around their necks, and mashed headband bows down between their ears. Straightening up, I felt pretty satisfied as the sun rose and bathed their goofy faces in dawn's soft, rose-pink glow. Last, but certainly not least, I fastened Duke's top hat to his handsome head.

With all my dancers costumed, I could take a moment to breathe and look around. Tractor owners in overalls and bandannas proudly polished their farm equipment to make them gleam. High schoolers in band uniforms wandered by to form up on the next street. Little girls in floaty polyester chiffon and curling iron–tight curls darted ahead of mothers trying to hair spray them. Beautiful women wearing sashes announcing their titles—Miss 4-H, Miss Volunteer Fire Department—glided by, yanking up their strapless gowns.

I was completely absorbed by this pre-parade parade. Big mistake. I didn't notice the police officer walking up the line of tractors and trailers behind us until I heard, "Good morning, miss." The man's deep voice was kind, but I about jumped out of my skin.

I pivoted to face him. "G-g-good m-morning, officer." I wanted to kick myself for stammering. Way to act nonchalant, Ariel.

"What a bevy of beauties," he said, reaching over the truck's side to rub under Midnight's chin.

"Yes, sir."

"Your inspection sticker has lapsed." He waited for me to answer, and when all I did was tremble like a leaf in a tempest, he must have figured he was scaring me. He lowered his voice a bit and spoke reassuringly. "I'm just checking everyone in the line here. It's a good time for us to catch out-of-date licenses and registrations. That's all. Where's your driver, sweetie?"

Where was she? I scanned up the street, down the street. No Sergeant Josie.

Slowly I turned back to the officer. "I—I—I . . ." I must have looked like those deer in our headlights that morning.

The man smiled encouragingly. "Maybe your driver went for coffee?"

I stood tongue tied.

Thank goodness, he wasn't one of those state patrol tough guys. I suppose they act so intimidating because they work the highways alone, the lone rangers of law enforcement. This man was donut-police, find-lost-children-in-shopping-malls helpful, that earnest grown-up Boy Scout type. Even so, I was so flipped out, I froze. Just like Sergeant Josie had said not to.

"To the Porta Potties, I bet?"

"M-m-maybe," I squeaked.

A hint of suspicion crept into the officer's expression. "Your truck's inspection sticker is almost a year overdue. Think you could reach into the glove compartment and pull out your registration? Do you know what I mean by 'registration'? It's a little card."

You know how dogs that care about you sense your emotions? My heart rate must have spiked because Duke decided I was in danger. He stuck his head out the rear cab window to growl—loud.

"Whoa now!" The officer stepped back. "Please control your dog, miss."

I reached in to scratch behind Duke's ears, which always quieted him. As I did, I realized I was basically pointing out more potential trouble: Duke had no collar, no dog tag.

The officer must have spotted that about the same time. He still tried to help: "Do you have a collar to put around Mr. Top Hat's neck, under that bow tie?"

"Back at the cabin, I think."

"What about the others? Wait a minute." Frowning, the policeman walked the length of the truck. "You have a lot of dogs back here, miss. They all yours?"

He turned to look at me. When I didn't answer, he shook his head, kind of sad, and reached to his waist for his walkie-talkie.

Oh God. Help, I thought.

I can't claim to know if my plea was actually answered or if it was just one of those fact-is-stranger-than-fiction moments, but I was saved by a Revolutionary War soldier! Honest to God. The biggest, brawniest man I'd ever seen—dressed in a frontiersman hunting shirt and breeches—stepped off the sidewalk curb and crushed the officer in a hug. "Fred! It is you. How are you, you old sinner?" He let go and held my interrogator at arm's length. "How long's it been, brother?"

The officer laughed and punched the frontier huntsman in the shoulder of his historically exact, fringed linsey-woolsey shirt. (What is it about guys hitting each other when they're glad to see one another?) "Too long, too long," he answered.

"I think it was when we had a little too much of the devil's drink in us. That time we went hooting 'n' hollering through town and got into a bit of a heated conversation with some bikers. Remember? Lordy, that was some night. Of course, I don't partake any more, now that I belong to Jesus. What about you, brother?"

The officer cleared his throat and looked around uncomfortably. "Not since I've put on the uniform." He put his arm over the reenactor's shoulders and walked him a couple of feet away. But I could still hear what he said next. "Wouldn't do me any good at the station to talk about the crazy moments of my youth. Know what I mean? Although it is good to see you, man."

The frontiersman nodded. "Understood, friend." He

hugged the officer again, who let out a big sigh of relief. "Now, what's going on here with Ariel and her ladies?"

This hulk of a man knew me? Somehow, I had the sense to keep quiet.

Since the Revolutionary War soldier knew who I was, the officer relaxed a bit. "I noticed the truck's inspection sticker is way past due, and the driver's not here," he explained. "The girl seems awful jittery. And then I started counting all these dogs. None of them on leashes, no tags. I remember something about the animal shelter being broken into. I was just going to run a check on the truck's tag to make sure nothing's up." He pulled the walkie-talkie off his belt.

The reenactor quick-glanced my way over his shoulder. I was about to burst into tears. All my hard work, my dream of showing that I could create something wonderful out of nothing, ruined. Because of a stupid sticker. Lo and behold—the guy winked at me.

Taking the officer by the arm, he said, "Awww, man, you got me. I've been having trouble with the missus, and I just keep forgetting to take care of chores. It's kind of hard for the two of us to see eye to eye these days, my having found salvation and her still counting on horoscopes to predict her path to the rapture. You know?"

"This your truck, then? Jes— Oh, sorry." The officer blushed, flustered that he'd almost cursed standing beside someone of faith. He cleared his throat. "For pity's sake, man, you forgot to get it inspected for a whole year?"

The frontiersman shrugged. "Arguments call for saying you're sorry and proving it with deeds. And truth be told, I have a lot to make up for. So I've been taking my lady out dancing a lot and repairing everything I can find that's broken around our place to prettify it for her. All on top of working my job at Walmart."

"Okay, Morgan. I hear you."

Morgan? Of course. Duh! This had to be Marcus's father! My heartbeat stopped pounding in my ears as I eased down a bit. If this man was anything like his son, I had some serious help standing in front of me.

Still, the policeman persisted. "But what about the dogs?"

"These dogs?"

"Yeah, Morgan. *These* dogs."

I waited, holding my breath.

"You know I've always hunted," said Marcus's dad, smooth as gelato. "Didn't we go out hunting together some as kids? Mostly I like pointers, you remember, but I bet these hounds would make fine trackers. Look at the size of their snouts." He laughed. "It turns out the dogs possess more talent than running down rabbits. Ariel"— he nodded in my direction—"has got them to dance. She thought they'd be a great addition to the parade." Not a single fib there.

"Dance? These mutts?"

"For sure. Lesser miracles have happened. Now, Fred, I've got my hunter's license right here," he reached toward his pocket. "Want to see that?"

"Naw." The officer waved him off. His walkie-talkie had started crackling with orders for him to head to the grandstand. "Just be sure none of those dogs jump off that truck into the crowd, you hear? And since I owe you more than one favor, just get that truck inspected first thing Monday morning." The officer tipped his hat at me and walked away.

I managed a wave goodbye, even though my knees felt like giving way beneath me.

Grinning, Marcus's dad lumbered over. He stuck out his hand to shake mine. I swear it was the size of a football.

"Thanks ever so much, Mr. Campbell," I gushed.

"No sweat. Marcus told me you might need help today. To speak God's truth, I don't care much for that family of yours. Your sister broke my boy's heart, and he's run off because of her. But he said you were jake. So I've been looking for you. Lucky the spirit had me in the right place at the right time. But there're no coincidences in life, you know."

He strolled around the truck and busted out belly laughing. "You have some foxy babes here, honey." The girls had crowded to the side to meet him. Dogs sure know dog people when they see them. "So, what's the plan? Where's your driver?"

"I don't know. She was here, then she wasn't." I scanned the street again for Sergeant Josie.

Marcus's dad was watching me closely. I knew he told his police officer buddy that he didn't believe in his wife's psychic powers, but some of them must have rubbed off on him because I swear he read my mind right then.

"Tell you what, Ariel. I don't feel like marching the parade today." He waved at some of his frontier brethren dressed in the same oatmeal-colored hunting shirts he wore as they passed by. He let them get out of earshot before adding, "I always get headaches marching with our fife and drum corps. They're loud enough to make Gabriel take his horn and run for cover. I love playing, but I prefer solo." He pulled a piccolo-like wooden fife out of his pocket. The instrument about disappeared in his strong hand. "You play?"

"Cello."

"Cello? Dang. Ain't you fancy?" But he winked at me again as he said it—just like Marcus would have. Then, putting that itty-bitty flute to his mouth, Marcus's dad whipped out an Irish gig, light and happy. The dogs pricked up their floppy, over-big ears. He stopped. "Mind carrying an extra passenger in that truck? If your driver isn't back by the time we need to roll, I can drive."

I couldn't believe how kind he was. "Oh, you're the best, Mr. Campbell. Just like Marcus."

Maybe he was right—maybe there aren't any coincidences, maybe things happened for a reason. But I sure couldn't tell you why I had to go through what happened next.

Sixteen

AROUND THE CORNER, MARCHING BANDS BEGAN to warm up. Tubas, trumpets, trombones tooted. Clarinets and saxophones zipped up and down their scales. Flutes and piccolos trilled. In a jumble of tunes, the musicians practiced the hardest measures of the Souza marches they'd be performing soon—just making sure their fingers still danced the melodies right.

Then the drum corps started.

BLAM, BLAM, BLAM, BLAM. A single snare drum beat out the 4/4 meter, and in an explosion of percussion, the other drums answered: RATTA-TAT-TAT, TATTA-RATTA-TAT. Cymbals, bass drums, tri-toms, snares. The loud rhythms bounced off the surrounding brick houses, the tight nineteenth-century streets acting like canyon walls to amplify the slamming drumbeats into echoing thunder.

My foot started tapping, my head bobbing. I'd always loved the way a drumline kicked me into wanting to move. I called up the memory of George strutting down those very streets in front of his marching band, his shoulders back and head high. He pumped his arms up and down to keep the beat steady so his musicians kept time together even when the band, marching in long rows, turned a corner so its front ranks were on a different street block from the back.

Another high school band felt the need to show off, too. Its drumline started up: BOOM-DE-BOOM-BOOM-BOOM.

RATTA-TATTA-TATTA-TAT.

Their competing drumbeats rumbled like cannon fire.

Smiling, revved by the music, I turned to Duke to tell him we'd be performing soon. But my words caught in my throat. Duke was hunched to the seat of the truck, trembling, his eyes wild.

"Oh no, boy, don't be afraid." I yanked open the truck door. That poor dog was shaking so hard his teeth were chattering. "It's just a band. Really, boy, it's all right." I hummed like I had before and hugged him tight, trying to push calm from my heart into his.

Duke actually began to ease down a little, whimpering with my humming. He was trying so hard to squash his fear, to trust me. But a third drumline decided to join the musical fray. BLAM-BLAM-BLAM-DIDEDAM.

With that, the combined drumbeats turned ear-splitting. The surrounding buildings pulsed with the beat. Just like a town would if its perimeters were under enemy fire. Just like I imagined an ambush battle might sound in Afghanistan.

It was too much for him. Terrified, Duke leaped out the open door and took off down the street.

"Go on!" Marcus's dad shouted at me. "I'll hold down the fort." He swung himself into the truck bed and gathered up all those princess dogs in his muscle-bound arms to keep them from chasing after me.

I hoisted my skirt and sprinted. "Duke," I called. "Duke, stop!"

Duke zigzagged low to the ground, from car to truck to lamppost to mailbox like soldiers do during a skirmish to confuse enemy gunmen. I could barely keep him in my sights. For a few minutes I could follow his top hat popping up and down as he darted through the crowds. But soon I had to track Duke more by seeing people lunge to the side, throwing their arms up in surprise and annoyance.

They were none too happy when a few seconds later I sideswiped them, too.

"Oh my Lord!" exclaimed ladies in pastel knit suits, strolling arm in arm with dapper old gentlemen in starched linen everything.

"Hey now!" grumbled ponytailed men holding hands with women in sparkle-studded jean jackets.

"Watch it!" shouted teenage boys with backward baseball caps and pants hanging off their butts.

It all glanced off me in my horror. I had to stop Duke before we got to the floats where G-L-O-R-I-A would be. He was already closing in on the patriotic ones built by the local VFW and Lions Club. I could see way down at the end of the street the floats for the queen and her princesses. Girls in gowns of pink and of green were already starting to arrange themselves on the wedding-cake tiers of the two matching princess floats. Their marine escorts helped them up the stairs.

Duke was heading straight for them.

"No!" I shouted. "Stop!"

But he didn't. Duke dove right underneath the first royal court float.

He disappeared with a swish of its glittery fringe, his top hat left spinning on the pavement.

I ran straight into the middle of those princesses, threw myself to the ground, and tried to crawl under the float after Duke.

I was halfway under when I heard some of those princesses shriek. "There's someone trying to get under the float!" Then the sound of running feet. Strong hands in white gloves grabbed my ankles and yanked me out to come nose to nose with spit-shined shoes. I gazed up into the faces of two young marines. They looked surprised. The half dozen princesses who quickly joined them looked disgusted.

Sweaty, dirty from the street, my hair all wacky, heaving to catch my breath from the chase, I probably looked horror movie–possessed, the craziest girl they'd ever seen live.

Ashamed, I stayed belly to the ground. All I could think to say was, "I'm looking for my dog."

"What?" Marines and princesses asked each other. "A dog; she said something about a dog," rippled from the front to the back of the group. I saw more sweeping skirts of green and of pink joining the circle.

"My dog. He ran under the float. The marching band drums scared him. I think he thought it was gunfire," I spoke my words to the shoes of the marines, hoping they'd understand. But I realized then they were cadets from the nearby Virginia military academy. They didn't know yet what Duke might be feeling, what Sergeant Josie or my brother might as well.

But one pink skirt seemed to. "Oh, poor dog. Drums sound just like thunder when they're playing in the street. The sound ricochets off the buildings and gets so amplified. I remember that from marching in the parade during high school."

"*Ooooooh.*" Girls' voices chorused. With that explanation, most of the pink skirts lost interest and drifted away. From the back of the crowd, I heard Gloria's voice: "Wow, that was so exciting the way you boys rushed to our defense. Does that mean you're our personal bodyguards?"

"If you want, ma'am," the cadet she was flirting with answered, and chuckled, their voices at a good distance now, obviously walking away.

I was left alone, save for the one friendly pink skirt. She knelt. "Can I help you get the dog out?"

That voice was really familiar, too. Slowly, terrified of Gloria still being close enough to see my face and recognizing that the insane girl was me, I raised my eyes. It was Emma. George's Emma.

I burst into tears. It was almost like finding George in this storm of troubles.

"Ariel!" Emma was just as stunned as I was. "Honey, what's the matter?" She helped me sit up.

I don't know how she understood what I was saying,

I was blubbering so much. But I told her how Duke had found me in a storm. How with music and dancing I'd helped him through what looked like PTSD. How I wanted to march in the parade with him, just like George and she had.

Emma wiped my face and smiled at me. "So let's get him out, okay?"

No wonder George loved her so much.

Lifting the float's skirts, Emma and I and peered into the cave-like dimness. I could see Duke cowering against one of its back wheels. If the float started to move, he'd be crushed. We needed to hurry. "Good boy. Come here, fella." I tried to croon and not sound like a tornado-warning siren in my urgency.

Duke just hid his face under his paws.

How I wished I had some bacon. I tried again. "It's all right. It's just drums. Come on."

Duke pulled his paws away from his face, at least.

"There," Emma said. "You'll get him. Try again."

I did. Duke listened, his tail starting to timidly tap the ground. But he didn't move.

"We're running out of time," I wailed. I could hear men with their megaphones calling to the floats to get ready.

"Let me try," said Emma. She whistled. "Come, boy. Come on. I want to meet you."

At the sound of Emma's voice, Duke's head popped up.

She whistled again. "Come on, sweet thing, you can do it."

He started to crawl.

I joined in, calling and whistling, patting the ground. "Come on, Duke. Come here, boy."

Duke scrambled out. He jumped on me and licked my face. Then he sat and laid his head on my knee, looking up and wiggling all over with his wagging, like he was apologizing for being such a dork.

Emma stroked his head. "What a beautiful dog, Ariel."

"Awwwwwwww." Suddenly we were surrounded again by princesses.

"What a darling dog!" "Oh, he's just precious." "Look at his bow tie and vest." "Is this his top hat?" "Oh my Gawd!"

Then they got a load of me. "Huuuuuhh?"

I looked down at myself. My beautiful emerald gown was smeared and torn. I couldn't perform like that. I'd be a total joke.

"Don't worry, Ariel." Emma squeezed my hand. "Ladies, what spare clothes do you have? Ariel has taught

this beautiful boy how to dance. Isn't that amazing?"
She waited for the answering "*Awwwww. That's so cute,*"
before going on: "They are going to dance in the parade."

"*Awwwwww.*"

"She needs to look as pretty as a princess."

There was a reason Emma was captain of the flag
corps when George was the drum major. Before I knew
what was happening, I was shoved into a Porta Potti
with an armload of clothes. For a moment I mourned
my grandmother's dress, the sense of being armed with
something belonging to that unmet, strong woman. But
today was about dance and choreography, I told myself,
what my imagination could do, not my dress. And it was
about to begin. No time to be sad—especially standing
in a plastic outhouse. I decided on a pink circle skirt and
black bolero jacket trimmed in pink braid—of all the
stuff the girls had handed me, it looked the most like a
dancer's.

Someone tamed my wildly disheveled hair into a thick
French braid, not unlike my grandmother's hairdo in
that photo. The hairdresser princess even pulled a few
apple blossoms from her own updo to tuck into my new
plaits.

Emma coaxed me into a little blush and lipstick for
the performance. "So people sitting in the back bleachers

can see your soulful face."

It was the sweetest and quickest makeover this side of *Seventeen* magazine. I didn't know girls that pretty could be that nice. I promised myself to remember that in the future and not judge them harsh or expect them to be mean just because they're beautiful.

The girls were clapping their hands in appreciation of me and themselves when a sharp voice stopped them: "What's going on?"

The princesses parted.

There stood G-L-O-R-I-A. Her mouth popped open at the sight of me.

"Look what we did!" "Doesn't she look apple-blossom lovely?"

Gloria started spluttering. "Ariel! What . . . what the . . . What are you doing here?"

Quick, Emma hugged me. "Time to exit," she whispered in my ear. "Shoo!" She gave me a little push and turned to herd the princesses. "We need to board our ship, ladies." She took Gloria by the hand and pulled her away.

Duke and I trotted down the street as everyone was scrambling to get onto their floats or turn on their engines. I looked back just once. Emma and Gloria were sitting together on the top tier of their princess float, in between two huge pink-and-white apple blossoms—the yin and the yang of princesses, if ever there were. Emma kinda glowed. Her smile radiated kindness. Gloria looked like the wrath of God.

She was sure to be gunning for me at the end of the parade.

Seventeen

MARCUS'S DAD WAS STANDING IN THE truck bed playing "Danny Boy" on his piccolo-fife when Duke and I made it back to the truck. I swear my girls were transfixed. But everyone is with that song; it's so beautiful and sad.

He stopped playing when he spotted me.

"Thanks for watching them, Mr. Campbell." I peeked in the truck cab. Still no Sergeant Josie. I tried not to worry, but the crowd was getting larger by the minute. I sure hoped she was okay and that the mass of parade-goers, their arms full now of bags and treasures from carnival booths, wouldn't trigger her leftover demons. "You really okay to drive us, Mr. Campbell?"

"Sure thang, miss." Pushing the seat back as far as it could go, he squeezed his Herculean self behind the steering wheel and turned the key. Luckily, Sergeant Josie had left it in the ignition. The tractors around us started up, too, backfiring in farts of smoke before settling into steady chugs and rattles.

Duke flinched and nudged his head under my hand for a reassuring pat. What an idiot I'd been not to think about how all this noise, the sudden bangs and drumbeats might scare him, just like I now realized they might Sergeant Josie. If he had been a military working dog, this was flashback city.

"That dog's been through some hell, hasn't he?" Marcus's dad commented. He reached for the glove compartment. "I found this when you were chasing him." He pulled out an envelope stuffed with bacon. "Will this help settle him? I'll do just about anything myself for some good bacon."

Sergeant Josie had thought of everything. She always did. Oh, I owed her so much. I felt awful. Had my asking her help and to bring me to the parade done something terrible to her? *Where was she?*

I knelt to talk to Duke, tapping into everything Sergeant Josie had taught me about training a dog. Not pity, empathy. Reassure but firmly. No-nonsense respect for his ability to tap into his own courage. Then praise when he managed it. I got Duke to sit. When he had stopped trembling entirely, I gave him a handful of bacon. "Good boy. It's time now, Duke. Time to show everyone what we can do. Okay? For me?"

I swear that dog took a deep breath and straightened himself up tall.

Maybe it was seeing Duke steel himself. Maybe it was watching Emma be so at ease squaring off with alpha girls like G-L-O-R-I-A. Maybe it was coming face to face with the moment that my BIG IDEA would either take flight or I'd fall flat on my face. But I felt the need to warn Marcus's dad that there could be trouble, BIG trouble, at the end of the parade. He needed to know how much of a tempest he was getting himself into.

"Pshaw, Ariel," he answered. "I survived Desert Storm. I survived being a drunk. I survive loving a woman who thinks if she concentrates hard enough she can call up ghosts. This ain't nothing, sugar."

He revved the engine. "Marcus would tell us to 'carpe diem.' Right?" He grinned. "Let's roll."

But trouble didn't wait for the end of the parade. It was already gathering itself and heading straight for us.

From one direction, I spotted Sergeant Josie hurrying toward the truck, carrying two Styrofoam cups. Ambling toward her was a group of guys holding their own cups of slushies. They looked ordinary enough—khakis, polo shirts, respectable haircuts, shaved baby faces. But they were laughing and making stupid and really offensive jokes about some of the women they saw.

They passed by the truck. "Jackasses," Marcus's dad muttered, hearing them. "Mind if I do a little proselytizing, Ariel? I feel some souls in need of saving from themselves."

But before he could open the truck door, the first one in that parade of jerks said, "Hey, look what's coming."

He was talking about Sergeant Josie.

He veered to head straight at her, knocking her shoulder to shoulder as he passed. Then he pivoted to stand right behind her. His posse encircled her. "Hey, Taco-head," he slurred. "You lost?"

Sergeant Josie stiffened.

Duke started to growl, low, in the back of his throat.

"Naw, she's not lost," said one of his bully buddies. "Bet she's one of them illegal immigrants."

"Bet she squirreled away somewhere after apple picking was over last fall, when all the other beaners traveled north following the crop season," said another.

"Yeah, and she's just now crawling out."

"Expecting to be taken care of by us hardworking Americans."

Marcus's dad struggled with the door to get out to help, but it stuck fast.

Sergeant Josie turned her head slightly to address the

guy standing behind her. "You're making a mistake, sir."

"Well, damn, boys. She's a polite little taco-head. Where you from, chiquita?"

The bully boys burst out laughing, sneering. She glared at them.

"I said where . . . are . . . you . . . from?" He moved in closer.

Sergeant Josie didn't flinch. "Puerto Rico."

"See, I told you!"

"Go back to your s**thole country, beaner." The guy parroted the awful label he'd heard the president use to demean foreign countries with citizens of color. Then he pushed her.

His buddies laughed again. Sergeant Josie held her ground. "Guess you flunked social studies. This *is* my country. And I've been serving it. Unlike you a-holes."

"Oh yeah?" The guy standing behind her grabbed her elbow. "So you're a mouthy Taco-head. I know some service you can do."

Marcus's daddy finally managed to shove the truck door open. He lunged out of the truck with a roar. "HEY! BACK OFF!" I see why people call on him to chase out demons. He was that intimidating when provoked by mean-spirited beings.

Duke also hurled himself through the open door,

growling and barking. I tumbled out to bring up the rear.

But before we could reach her, Sergeant Josie had her assailant on his knees immobilized, holding one of his arms twisted behind his back. His drink was spilled in a slick of sticky-sweet blue ice, slowly mixing with her black coffee and a milky-white hot chocolate she must have been bringing for me.

He was sniveling. "Get this"—I shouldn't say what awful thing he called her—"off me!"

Throwing their drinks to the ground, his *Lord of the Flies* pack started to close in on her.

Until Marcus's dad reached them. Boy, did they scatter then, especially as Duke rushed to Sergeant Josie's side. He barked ferociously at the man she'd pinned, all the fur along his spine raised. He'd have been scary as a hellhound except for that top hat I'd put on him that popped up and down as he barked.

Even so, her assailant cowered and whimpered. Sergeant Josie held on to him.

"This blockhead is not worth it, ma'am," Marcus's dad said to her. "Trust me."

Sergeant Josie didn't let go. Her expression was battle-ready fierce.

Marcus's dad looked over his shoulder at the crowd

and then back to her. "There are a whole lot of cops round here, ma'am. They shouldn't, but they might listen to this idiot. Any claims he might want to make. About you. About what happened. You don't want to miss today sitting in their holding cell. I've been there myself and I can tell you the view stinks."

"Parade starting in five minutes. Five minutes! Everyone to their floats!" a megaphoned voice called.

Sergeant Josie looked up at Marcus's dad. Slowly, the righteous fury on her face dissipated. "I see you brought reinforcements," she said to me.

After another moment of consideration, she let go of her attacker with Avenger-heroine professionalism.

He fell flat to the ground, cursing all sorts of things. "I'm not finished with you yet," he sniped.

"Oh, but you know what . . . sir . . . I'm done with you." She patted Duke. "Thanks, buddy," she whispered in his ear. Stepping over her assailant, Sergeant Josie introduced herself to Marcus's dad.

Then she looked at me and smiled. "Don't you have a parade to get to?"

If you've never seen a parade live—felt the street throb and your heart pulse in rhythm with a passing band's drum cadence, been swept up in all the colors and confetti and celebration—promise yourself to do it before you die.

Better yet, march in one.

As soon as we reached the parade start point and fed into that stream of music and excitement, we all came alive. Marcus's dad had joined Sergeant Josie in the truck and Duke and I marched right in front of it, like George leading his band. And just like George, Duke strutted confidently. Armed with music, he seemed to have no fears. He was *invulnerable.*

Me? I made myself stop thinking. I had an hour of joy ahead of me. For one hour, I was going to live a philosophy from one of my collected quotes: love as if no one had ever hurt me, dance as if there was no one out there to judge me, live as if this moment was a little bit of heaven right here on earth.

I'd made a playlist on my cell phone that we'd tapped into Sergeant Josie's truck radio with an auxiliary chord. It was pretty jerry-rigged, and my old phone's juice would just barely last the length of the parade. But I couldn't worry over things like that anymore. When Sergeant Josie cranked up the volume and Stevie Wonder's lyrics—about the power of music to envelop and move us—filled the street, Duke and I became song in motion.

"You can feel it all o-o-o-ver. You can feel it all over, people."

Walk, spin, stop, shake. Circle, serpentine, kick, bow.

We were marching at the parade's tail end, after the more serious floats and city hall dignitaries had long passed by. After the queen and her princesses. After the NFL stars. After the fire trucks. After the marching bands. After the fife and drum corps. After the circus clowns. And after the Harley-Davidsons. So the crowd was loosened up and pumped to have some fun.

Walk, spin, stop, shake. Circle, serpentine, kick, bow.

I was vaguely aware of a sea of pink and green hats and scarves. Then I heard clapping and cheering and realized that all those faces were smiling, the people watching us were keeping the beat with us.

"Awwww, look at the Fred Astaire dog!"

"Oh my Gawd, he can dance."

"Mommy, can we teach Spot to dance, too?"

Then the crowd actually began singing along in unison: "WE can feel it all o-o-o-ver!"

It was beyond sweet.

But that reaction was nothing compared with what happened when Midnight and her court had their moment in the spotlight. I knew I'd picked the perfect music for my rambunctious dogs, but I guess "Express

Yourself" just appeals to everyone's pent-up creative urges. From the moment the sounds of Charles Wright and the Watts 103rd Street Rhythm Band boogied into the air and my ladies started to jive to the funk song, we owned our part of that parade.

I had managed to synchronize a few of my girls' movements. As Wright sang, *"Express yourself!"* my escapee dogs swayed and "sang" like a backup girl chorus. "Bark, bark," they answered him, yapping on beat with the trumpets and saxophones, and turning their heads— left, right, left, right—to the 4/4 rhythm.

Mostly, though, the girls freestyled. When Wright sang, *"It's not what you look like when you doin' what you're doin',"* the ladies jumped up and moved however they wanted. Kep spun round. Bodger panted like she was lip-synching. Lassie wagged her tail so her butt sashayed in time (almost!) to the music. Jump hopped up and down. Duchess put her front paws atop the truck bed's railing and patter-stepped along it like she was playing a piano.

Midnight simply nodded her head regally until the finale. When the 103rd Street Band instrumentalists jammed and Wright scat-sang and then repeated over and over, *"Express yourself!"* Midnight stood and turned around, her pink tutu swinging prettily. She barked in a friendly way at the crowd, like she was encouraging them to join in.

Danged if some people didn't take her up on the invitation to express themselves, too! I could hardly believe it. The very first person to step out of the crowd onto the street pavement to join in our little parade was Ms. Math, my algebra teacher, carrying a poodle she'd dyed pink for the Festival. I kid you not. She fell in behind Sergeant Josie's red truck and swung that poodle back and forth in time to the funk beat. I'd never seen her smile that big—not even as she speed-solved the trickiest of equations at the whiteboard!

I'd timed the playlist to alternate between Wonder and Wright for the fifty minutes it would take us to march the entire length of the parade, so Duke and I could switch off with the girls. "Express Yourself" played eight times over as we snaked through the parade route. By the time we'd reached the grandstand, we had two dozen dogs and their owners trailing us.

Old, young; tall, short; graceful, gangly; dignified, ridiculous. They did their own versions of the twist, the Macarena, the pony, the polka. One lady did "the bump," that silly seventies dance, crashing her bottom against her Great Dane's side every other beat. Another woman tried some Irish step dance, her red setter nipping at her feet.

As we neared the grandstand, people started pointing, then they laughed and cheered as loud as if we were in the final minutes of a tied football bowl game. Local TV cameras whipped around to film whatever was causing the commotion. I could barely hear Stevie's music over it all. I dared to look up into the stands, hoping to see Daddy with the courthouse crowd. There he was, sitting right behind the mayor. Hopping up and down on my tiptoes, I waved both arms at him. He stood and cheered. At me! Daddy!

And would you believe, everyone sitting in the stands waved back at me, too, like I was a Hollywood star or something.

All I can say is there have to be a lot of frustrated dancers out there in the world—people who are dying to express themselves, to let out their creativity in whatever way they can. I'd never imagined that my little moment of flight could nudge others into testing their own wings.

Of course all that was about to crash-land. At the end of the block, where the parade concluded and each marching group disbanded, I could see G-L-O-R-I-A. She stood with her arms crossed, smoldering thunder in her face. Beside her was Mama, like a towering cumulonimbus cloud of outrage. And beside her—a sheriff's deputy.

Eighteen

THE STORM BEGAN WITH JUST A rumble. You know, the kind of thunder you hear in the distance as dark clouds are gathering but which might slide by you if you're lucky. Or like the warning growl of a dog you might be able to calm down with a treat.

"Miss," the deputy addressed me. He had the same kind of helpful smile the police officer who'd been checking inspection tickets had had earlier. Maybe I could talk my way out of this typhoon of trouble somehow. Coming off that parade, I thought anything was possible. "Did you have a permit to march in the parade?" he continued. "I didn't see this float described on the list."

A dozen answers quick-flashed through my head. But I decided on honesty and keeping a lid on my usual angsty defiance. "No, sir, I didn't. I'm sorry. Is that a problem?"

"Well, yes, it is, miss." The deputy glanced at Duke, then up at my conga-line girls. At the sight of them, he fought off a smile. I could see it. He must be a dog lover. I had a chance.

"Oh gosh," I said, and started to claim I didn't know that not registering beforehand was a problem. But that was a fib. "Can I fill out an application now?"

"I'm afraid not." He thought a moment. "Maybe we can deal with this with a fine and a ticket of some kind."

"Wait! That's it? You're not going to arrest her or something?" Gloria and Mama shouted at the deputy, in unison—I swear—just like always.

And there it was: the first zap of serious lightning, sizzling across the scene.

"She's a thief." Gloria kept up the salvo. "Those are my clothes!" She pointed to my princesses. "My sweaters. My ribbons. My headbands. Ohhh—my tutu!"

"Your sister taking some of your outfits out of her own home isn't enough for me to arrest her," the deputy cautioned Gloria.

"Well, what about those dogs? I know she stole them. She and Marcus went to the shelter the day they disappeared. She told me they were going to take them."

"I did not!" I cried.

At the mention of Marcus, I felt his dad get out of

the truck and stand behind me—a total reincarnation of that legendary stand-down-an-army frontiersman, that scary-accurate rifleman Daniel Morgan. But even that didn't stop Gloria.

"I bet she stole other things. I bet she took money. She acts so weird all the time, she's capable of anything! Right, Mama?"

"I have no control over Ariel," Mama said. "She ruins everything. I am ashamed to call her mine, officer."

My own mother said that. It's not that I couldn't believe it—that was precisely what she'd always made me feel and what I suspected she thought. The fact she would hurl such a hurtful truth in front of so many people didn't surprise me either. She probably figured everyone would take one look at me and sympathize with her.

But I just couldn't stand it anymore. Not after the triumph, the thrill of that parade. Not after showing everyone what my imagination, the music inside my soul, could do. I felt a tsunami of pent-up hurt and frustration build in me. I started to scream how bad she made me feel, every single day. But in the corner of my eye, I caught the movement of Sergeant Josie opening the truck door and rising out of her seat. My mind flashed back to how she'd handled those racist boys calling her names. She'd kept cool. Collected. Even under fire.

So I stood my ground, tilting my chin—that juts out anyway like I'm looking for a fight—in a go-ahead-hit-me-and-see-what-happens stance and waited. But I wasn't above throwing one verbal punch at Gloria—for Marcus. Just loud enough for her to hear, I said, "At least I don't dump really nice boyfriends just because they don't fit my princess image."

Gloria actually blushed hot red. A moment of regret? Self-recognition? Or just fury? I'll never know for sure because the next thing she did was grab me by my French braid. I twisted away, but she hung on and I swung us around—like I was one of those marlin fish Hemingway always wrote about battling to reel in. We toppled to the ground, all tangled together, Gloria swatting at me.

"Hold on!" The deputy tried to drag Gloria off me.

Mama actually shoved him. He fell on top of us. "Stay out of this!" Mama shouted at him, and then leaned over to hiss at me, "Just wait till I get you home."

All H-E-double hockey sticks broke loose then. My princess pooches didn't like Gloria manhandling me. They started barking and howling.

Sergeant Josie jumped out of the truck to quiet them. Marcus's dad waded into the battle and in one lift picked the deputy off the ground to stand on his feet. The officer went after Mama while Marcus's dad pried

Gloria's hands from my hair. Freed from her clutches, I took a swing at Gloria, knocking us all back down into a flailing heap. In the scuffle, I ended up at the bottom of the pile.

One after another, Lassie, Bodger, Jump, Duchess, and Kep dove off the truck and came to my rescue. Dividing themselves as if on a coordinated commando raid, Lassie bit onto the pants-seat of the officer while Bodger grabbed Mama's skirt to tug and tug to pull the humans apart. It took three dogs—Duchess, Jump, and Kep—yanking on the breeches of Marcus's dad to move him. With them pulled away, Gloria and I came up from the ground, still slapping at each other, just as the deputy's pants ripped open to his ankles.

That's about the time the TV crews started filming the fracas.

Two more officers came running. One of them clutched a dog-catcher's noose. Oh no! I panicked. Duke! Midnight! The girls! I was so distracted, Gloria landed a shove that knocked me flat.

At that, Duke flew into action. He stood over me and barked at Gloria, urgent but not threatening. Like, *Hang on a minute!* When she froze, surprised, Duke stopped barking. He whined a little and cocked his head at my sister.

Gloria just stared at him.

Duke turned to woof once at Mama, then whined and cocked his head at her. Mama stopped whacking at the police officer and stared.

My princess dogs sat down, too, one after another, as if cued by a stage manager. The deputy grabbed his belt loops and pulled his pants together. Marcus's dad got back on his feet. Midnight finally slid herself off the truck and came to Sergeant Josie, leaning against her leg and gazing up at her, as if asking what in the world was going on.

There was a bizarre silence.

Into the middle of all that Daddy came running, all excited. "Ariel, honey, that was amazing!" He swept me up in a hug. "So that's what you were doing in the basement. I'm so proud of you!"

Like I said before, Daddy is in his own head a lot. It took him a few seconds to figure out something pretty bad was going on.

"Anything wrong, officer?" he asked.

"Wrong?" The poor man was trying to hold on to some semblance of authority as he gripped the shreds of his pants. "There sure as heck is something wrong." He turned to the two other officers. "Arrest the lot of them! Impound those dogs!"

I hadn't realized it, but my fellow dancers, the spectators who'd joined our little parade of self-expression, were standing around us in a circle that was growing bigger by the minute. I caught my math teacher's eye as the police hurried toward my princesses. I'm not sure if that woman had a moment of pity, a desire to help a kid in distress, or if her reaction had more to do with her being one of those fanatical dog lovers. Anyone who'd dye a poodle pink had to be a little obsessed, right? But whatever her motivation, I will be forever grateful for what she did next.

"Officers, stop." She stepped in front my girls. "I'd like to adopt this dog." She put her hand on Lassie's head. "And make a donation to the shelter in her name. Can you tell me who to make the check out to?"

"Oh, I can, darlin'!" An exquisitely chic Junior League–type lady waved her pink-gloved hand. "I'm on the board for the local ASPCA." People parted to let her through. In her pearls, lime-green designer suit, and kitten heels of the same color, no one would argue with her. "Any other takers?" She'd obviously run many a charity auction. "Take a dog and support humane treatment of animals!"

"This one's mine," Sergeant Josie said quietly but

very firmly, resting her hand on Midnight, stopping the approach of a young couple dressed in matching pink seersucker. They chose Kep instead, who looked like she was going to lift off the ground, her tail was propeller-wagging so fast.

One of the church ladies—who sang with the choir—came forward. Jump picked *her*—bounded right up to that woman and gave her one of those growly, musical talking-tos that dogs do when they really want people to listen. That church lady just melted. They sashayed away together, Jump bark-crooning in answer to that lady talking to her in singsongy voice: "Friend, tell me all those troubles. Oh my goodness, really? I hear you, baby. Have a few sorrows of my own. I'll share your load." Their conversation sounded just like the lyrics to that song "Lean on Me," I swear.

Within a few minutes, every one of those thrown-away dogs had a new loving home, just as Marcus and Sergeant Josie and I had hoped.

"Wait," Gloria wailed. "My clothes!"

The new owners stripped their dogs, chucked the clothes at Gloria, and disappeared into the crowd with the Junior League lady. When Gloria held a bundle of pink and green in her arms, she wailed even louder. "They're all stretched out!"

"Shut up, Gloria," Mama snapped. "There are TV cameras here. Wipe your face."

My princesses might be safe, but the maelstrom wasn't over yet.

Mama turned to the deputy. "What are you going to do about Ariel? She ruined the parade."

Daddy gasped. "Delilah! What are you doing?"

"E-e-eddie! This was Gloria's chance to be seen by talent agents. Now they're all distracted by this mess Ariel's caused. She's ruined our best bet for getting to Hollywood!"

"*Our?*" Daddy looked baffled.

"Well, none of you are going anywhere anytime soon," interrupted the deputy. "I'm taking you in for disorderly conduct and resisting arrest."

"Hey, Frank. I came to your aid, buddy," Marcus's dad defended himself. Did he know all the county cops? I wondered.

"Not you, Morgan." He turned and motioned to his fellow officers. "Arrest these women."

"Oh my, I feel faint." Mama started to wobble at the knees.

Following Mama, Gloria gasped, "Goodness, me too!" She managed to drop her armload of clothes, so the two of them fell into the heap of pink and green. All caught on camera so handcuffing them would look like police brutality, for sure.

But hauling me off would seem right appropriate since I still didn't know better than to spit into the wind. I stood defiant, in a go-ahead-I-dare-ya glare, holding on to Duke by his bow tie—the picture of a bound-for-H-E-double-toothpicks, unrepentant storm-child.

The officers started for me. Duke growled at them.

"Someone get a muzzle and control noose for that dog!"

I started to look to Sergeant Josie to save me—again. But I realized that I'd conjured up this storm. I had to quiet it myself.

I dropped to my knees and wrapped my arms tight around Duke. "No, you can't take him. He's just looking out for me. I think he might be an old army K-9 dog. They trained dogs to protect and defend, you know. I bet he's a war hero."

I looked up to the deputy clutching his pants. "I'm sorry if I caused trouble, officer. I didn't mean to. This dog had PTSD from something pretty bad. But I discovered that music was healing for him and helped him stay calm and be brave. Then I found out that people actually train dogs to dance. It's all over YouTube. You can check it out yourself. Soooo"—I stammered a bit in

daring to reveal my hopes—"I—I—I wanted to show off what my imagination could do. And—and —and—"
There was nothing to do but be pinkie-swear honest. "I did want to steal some of the spotlight from Gloria."

"See! What did I tell you?" Mama began to rant. "She needs a serious lesson! She should be—"

"Please," Daddy interrupted, "let her talk, Delilah." Unbelievably, Mama stopped, midsentence. Daddy had never—ever—asked her to stop talking. Not for me anyway.

I raced on: "But that was just at the beginning. I discovered that I could actually create something epic, something wondrous, a straight-from-the-heart outcry, something bursting with joy. No matter what people say about me."

I felt myself searching all the faces watching me as I spoke. "I learned that if we listen, *really* listen, we can find such soul-lifting music. In ourselves. In each other. Even . . . even in a storm. Like—like the finale of Beethoven's 'Ninth.' It starts out all angsty with the string basses rumbling like thunder. And then suddenly the woodwinds come in, light and hopeful, like a sun-break in storm clouds, like . . . like a catbird after a rain."

Realizing I had gotten a little geeky, I pointed to my princesses. "Did ya'll see how beautiful these mutts could be when they soaked up the music and danced?"

"Oh, I did!" "Ain't it the truth!" "Amen, sister!" people in the crowd shouted.

I turned to my father. "Please, Daddy. I don't care if they arrest me. But please don't let them take Duke. I think he might have served in Afghanistan, just like Sergeant Josie." I nodded toward her. "Just like George."

Maybe it was the mention of George, maybe it was my acting less selfish. Daddy kicked into his legendary defense-attorney mode, the daddy I'd been so proud of, the daddy George had loved talking to. "Officer," he said, "did you tell my wife and daughters that they were under arrest before you laid a hand on them?"

"Why, I . . . I must have," the deputy blustered.

"Mmmmmm, no you didn't, Frankie," said Marcus's dad.

"I see." Daddy clasped his hands behind his back and paced a bit. "They didn't know you intended to arrest them, since you failed to state it, therefore, they couldn't have been resisting. In fact, it seems to me that any disorderly conduct resulted from your instigation. They acted in self-defense." He swept his hand toward the onlookers, recognizing a friendly jury when he saw it. "I dare say any one of us might have reacted in the very same way."

The crowd nodded.

The deputy scowled. "No way! Those girls threw punches at each other. The princess"—he pointed to Gloria—"grabbed that one"—he pointed to me—"by the hair."

"Ariel, do you wish to press charges against Gloria?"

I could see where Daddy was going with all this. "No, sir."

"There's the matter of the stolen dogs, then," the policeman tried.

"What dogs?"

The sheriff searched the crowd in vain. "*Hmpf*, well, that dog, then." He pointed at Duke.

"He wasn't at the pound!" I blurted out. "Only girl dogs were taken."

"AHA! How would you know that unless you were at the scene of the crime?" The deputy pointed at me, letting one of his torn-up pant legs fall.

"Don't answer that, Ariel," Daddy told me. He pressed his lips together to keep from laughing at the officer's exposed boxers—they were dotted with little police cars!

He waited for the deputy to get himself covered up— muttering "my wife gave me these"—before continuing. "We've all heard the news reports about the shelter break-in. So it stands to reason that Ariel would know that detail.

"Madam," Daddy called into the crowd to the animal shelter board lady, "were any army dogs, male, reported missing? You swear to tell the truth now?"

"Yes, sir. I always tell the truth. And no, sir, there were no male dogs missing."

"There now." Daddy smiled, and using the court of public opinion to pressure the sheriff, he said, "In the spirit of the Festival, of spring and new beginnings, can't we just let all this go so everyone can enjoy this day of celebration and promise?"

I thought the deputy might explode, he was so frustrated. But when the crowd started cheering and clapping, he had no choice but to agree.

Oh, it was a masterful performance by Daddy. So was the next thing he did. I could see how good he must be in court defending his clients. Daddy took Gloria's hands and said quietly, "Embrace your sister and make up. That's what a real princess would have the grace to do."

"Oooooh, Ariel." Gloria fluttered her hands around her cheeks as if she were fighting back tears. "I'm sooooo sorry." She grabbed me for a huge kissy hug.

The TV cameras caught that, too. And do you know

a talent scout handed Gloria his business card right afterward?

Before Mama could start in on me, Daddy said, "I think we should be proud of both our daughters, Delilah. After all, you're their mama." He smiled, and for a second, I saw exactly what those old women meant about his being a handsome, charming devil.

I could hardly believe it, but it was true. Daddy had taken my side in a family feud, for the very first time. He knelt beside Duke and me so I could hear him over the crowd jabbering and applauding what they'd just witnessed. "That was quite a ballet you just choreographed for all of us," he said. "You know who would have loved that?"

"George?" I asked hopefully.

"Oh, for sure, George, honey." His eyes welled up behind his horn-rimmed glasses. "I was also thinking of your grandmother. She always loved good, give-it-all-you-got drama! She would have been very proud of you. Just like I am."

He gave me a hug, and Duke squeezed right in there with us.

Coda

I'D LIKE TO TELL YOU IT was all smooth sailing around here after that. But storms sometimes subside slowly, leaving a lot of rubble in their wake that has to be cleared away.

The ride home was pretty rough—plenty of accusations splashing around between Gloria and me—although it helped to have Duke sitting between us. In the end, that business card from the talent scout quieted Gloria as she held it tight and imagined and imagined. She didn't even seem to notice Duke drooling down the back of her princess dress as he stuck his nose up against her cracked-open window to happily suck in the 55 mph winds Daddy's Cadillac was making.

Daddy kept going on and on about how wonderful, how clever, my dog dancing had been. He called me "our own little Martha Graham" and then had to explain to

Mama who she was. When Mama got squirmy listening to all this praise of me, Daddy won his case by saying how much I was starting to remind him of Mama, given how talented and all I'd become. I'm not sure either Mama or I particularly cared for that compliment.

However, soothed by Daddy's flattery, Mama just silently stewed for the rest of the way home. So I got to replay the glory of the day over and over in my mind, grinning as big as a panting dog after a good game of catch.

But that smile was wiped off my face fast as soon as we drove into our lane. In front of our house was a black Ford four-door, the kind of car army officers drive to deliver bad news.

I don't always find God—or a higher-power whatever—where I'm supposed to. Sometimes I hear it in music, sometimes I see it in apple blossoms, sometimes I feel it in dance, and sometimes I catch the cool awakening promise of it in the winds as they brush my face. Other times I can't believe he or she or it exists at all: things can go so bad here on earth.

But that day something merciful was at work. George wasn't dead.

He was hurt, though. Out on patrol, George had

spotted children in a field, trying to play soccer with a can. He wanted to give them the Beanie Babies I'd sent and told his driver to pull over. They hit an IED buried by the roadside—one of those handmade, improvised explosive devices Sergeant Josie had described that have been the number one killer of our soldiers in Afghanistan. The very hidden dangers that working dogs like Sergeant Josie's risk their lives to sniff out. When George's Humvee hit that bomb, it was thrown up and flipped in midair by the blast, hurling its passengers clear of the fire that quickly consumed it. Remarkably, no one died—not even the children running toward the car to get the toys. But they were all wounded, and George's legs were pretty mangled.

Daddy's over with George now, at a military hospital where doctors piece soldiers back together before sending them home to the States. Daddy emailed me that George is awful confused from the concussion and real jumpy when the nurses walk by with the rolling tray of meds. But Daddy's main news was that the very first smile they've gotten out of George was when Daddy showed him a YouTube video of Duke and me dancing at the parade.

I don't have the right words to explain how that made me feel.

I emailed Daddy back and promised that I'd work real hard to help George get better when he comes home. Duke had showed me how.

Daddy wasn't the only one to find that YouTube clip. It's already gotten over a million hits! Even Marcus, on the run, saw it. He wrote me a postcard from Ashville, North Carolina: *Way to go, Ariel. Those girls sure cut a rug.* I hope he comes back home someday.

The boy with the big gleaming grin saw it, too. He told me so when he sat down beside me (Me!) on the bus the other day. He was holding a copy of Jack London's *Call of the Wild* and started telling me all about the book. "The dog in it is half Saint Bernard and half shepherd. It made me think of your dog. Wanna borrow it when I'm done?" he asked.

"I do," I said, without even dropping my mouth open in surprise. Can you believe it?

There are always a few reporters from DC who come out to cover the parade, its celebration of "Americana" and "old-fashioned" sense of community. Typically, they find the grittiest or most eccentric thing to photograph and write up. This year, that was me. A *Washington Post* reporter did a bunch of interviews and then wrote a blurb that ended: "This little canine choreographer is going places." I'm going to frame that clip and hang it in my bedroom as a real pick-me-up on rainy days.

Thanks to all the publicity, the shelter's received a bunch of donations and may host summer camps featuring dog dancing. They want Duke and me to perform at them. That'll be way cool.

For a while, I was sort of worried Gloria might want to smother me in my sleep because of the attention I was getting. But things have changed between us. Now that I can define myself on my own terms a little better, now that I've imagined and created my own melody, people not understanding me or mistakenly labeling me just doesn't hurt as much. I know who I am. Just like George once said to me: "Music can overcome everything, change everything—that's what I love about it. Understand?"

I do now. It'll be one of the first things I tell George when he gets home.

Gloria's hit pay dirt herself. That talent scout who saw her at the parade, the one who gave her his card? He's gotten her cast in a new reality show. Gloria is heading to Hollywood—*without* Mama. Gloria actually grinned when she told me that part of the news and has been real friendly to me since. Only now do I see that maybe she was too overwhelmed by Mama to express herself. And that maybe Gloria didn't like being defined and predicted by other people either.

Including me. When I told her that I'd come to that realization and apologized and then promised to try to stop being mad at her for being born pretty, Gloria gave me a real hug, not one of those for-show princess ones. As she did, she whispered in my ear—so we didn't have to look each other straight in the eye, not yet anyway—that she'd try to stop being mad at me for being born "so damn smart." Gloria even drove me to the county registrar so I could buy a dog license for Duke to make him officially mine.

She also stood by me as the vet checked for an identification chip that could take Duke away from me. She noticed I was literally holding my breath and turning sort of blue. "Breathe," she whispered. But she sighed in relief along with me when the vet finished running that wand along Duke's body and found nothing clearly marking him as belonging to the military.

On the drive home, Gloria burbled on and on about Hollywood as Duke leaned forward from the back seat and put his head on the armrest so I could pat him. She was leaving in two weeks.

"Hey, Ariel?" She was suddenly serious.

"Yeah?"

"Promise to keep me up on how George is when he gets home?"

I promised. And like I said, I always keep my promises. Maybe Gloria and I can find our sisterhood in texts and emails about someone we both love.

Mama? She agreed to letting me keep Duke, but I don't know what's in store for Mama and me long-term. Sometimes opposites just have to coexist side by side without really understanding one another, I suppose. Ominous rain clouds jammed up on a bright shaft of sunshine make rainbows, right? Even if just for a few seconds.

Right now Duke and I are going outside. Sergeant Josie and Midnight are coming to pick us up for a picnic. She's decided to stay in her cabin for now. I'm so glad she's not leaving. She's working on desensitizing herself by helping a group train dogs to be companions for wounded veterans who are having a hard time readjusting to civilian life. Midnight goes to those sessions, too, and follows one step behind Sergeant Josie wherever she goes. She makes Sergeant Josie laugh—a lot more than she did before. These days, her refrigerator is stuffed full with bacon.

A quick-hit thunder-gusher just banged through here, and I can smell the old-timey peonies opening up, the ones my grandmother planted outside my window, their sweet scent spilling along those warm breezes that push away a spring storm. I don't mind saying it's a truly G-L-O-R-I-O-U-S scent.

The hills to the west are covered with apple trees blooming for all they're worth. On bad days, I will conjure up the image of those brave, brash little trees surviving the harshest change-of-season storms: brutal gales, merciless hail, a cacophony of thunder, and tidal waves of nightmare clouds. Surviving to throw open pink blossoms in poetical defiance of all the forces that had raged against them. I can hardly wait to taste their sweet-tangy, crisp apples come fall.

Duke is sitting, leaning all over me, snuffing in the world. I'd love to know if he can name to himself all the smells he's so enjoying. We've tried—truly—but haven't found out where he came from or what hardships he had to endure before finding me sobbing atop a mountain. I guess I'll never know if Duke was trained to find danger in doorways or if someone cruel had kicked him through one too many times.

What I do know for certain is that he came to me in a storm, the gift of wild winds and to-the-soul rattling thunder, and taught me to dance.

AUTHOR'S NOTE

I need to thank my oh-so-astute and incredibly nurturing editor, Katherine Tegen, for her faith in me, and my poetic children—my creative muses and unofficial first editors—for encouraging me to spread my own wings with Ariel's narrative.

Hopefully, *Storm Dog* has left you with many thoughts, yearnings even, and questions. One of the great joys in writing is that an individual story can open windows to many topics and themes, like those *National Geographic* magazine covers that captivate Ariel and introduce her to dog dancing.

If you're interested in learning a little more about Military Working Dogs; K-9 trainers; rescue pets; dog dancing; dogs helping veterans suffering PTSD; and the real-life artists like Martha Graham mentioned in this novel, please visit my website www.lmelliott.com. I'll be posting articles and bios (including some about famous MWDs like Cairo, who accompanied SEALs on the Osama bin Laden raid), plus photos of places like Sky Meadows State Park, recordings of catbirds and peepers, links to resources, and a few discussion questions you might want to consider. You'll also find Ariel's playlist of songs—so you can hear and dance to all of them yourself. I'll also share her and Sergeant Josie's favorite book recommendations, with a little poetry added in for fun.

A few words here, however, on some extraordinary beings: those MWDs. Dogs have served armies for centuries, as long ago as the Roman Empire. The United States has enlisted their aid since the American Revolution as sentries, scouts, and messengers, but did not formally train them for active duty until World War II. These days, the US military has about 2,500 working dogs serving here and abroad—as many as 600 were deployed in Afghanistan and Iraq during the most intense fighting of those wars.

Currently, new dogs are trained at Lackland Air Force Base, Texas, in an intense, painstaking three-month program that determines which specialty suits them best: patrol, detection, or tracking. From there, they go on for further training with chosen handlers. The program produces about 270 dogs a year. But only half who enter that initial training will graduate, proving they have the life-or-death necessary personality traits, endurance, devotion to duty, and responsiveness to human partners. It is a high bar for any dog (or human for that matter) to reach. Being too playful, for instance, might disqualify a dog, or wilting in one-hundred-degree-plus heat, or getting too agitated at the sound of gunfire.

Most MWDs are German Shepherds or Belgian Malinois, but sporting dogs like retrievers are particularly gifted in search-and-rescue missions or tracking someone building and planting IEDs. In addition to guarding bases and sweeping vehicles entering a compound, MDWs go out on patrol, where they and their handlers search for hidden, buried explosives by walking at the head of an infantry unit, making themselves easy targets for enemy snipers. High winds and brutal heat all dilute or confuse scents. Even then, dogs remain up to 100,000 times more alert to smells than humans. In 2010, after spending almost $19 billion and four years researching technology that could locate IEDs, a Pentagon task force concluded it couldn't invent anything as effective or reliable as these amazing dogs.

MWDs are also trained to attack enemy combatants if necessary. Handlers recount hundreds of incidents of their canine partners saving both their lives and entire platoons. Some working dogs have even been awarded medals for their valor, including one named Remco, who received a Silver Star for charging an insurgent's hideout in Afghanistan. Such bravery is the stuff of military legend, as is MWDs' devotion to those they love. There are many a heart-wrenching story of dogs shielding their handlers from gunfire or refusing to leave their side when their human partners are injured during a battle.

Tragically, for decades—out of fear they could not adjust to a retired civilian life—these canine heroes were euthanized after their service. Thankfully, in 2000, Congress passed the Robby Law, named for a Marine Corps working dog, which allows retired MWDs to be adopted. Most go home with one of their handlers, although carefully screened civilians can adopt them as well.

(The current wait to adopt a MWD is eighteen months. On any given day across the country, six million rescue animals wait in shelters, hoping for a forever family. Perhaps you will take one to your heart soon.)

Sergeant Josie, by the way, is representative of some of our finest veterans—female K-9 handlers and Puerto Rican service men and women. Puerto Ricans have been American citizens since 1917, when President Woodrow Wilson signed the Jones-Shafroth Act. They have been serving our nation ever since: 65,000 during World War II, 61,000 in Korea, 48,000 in Vietnam, and some 35,000 currently in active duty. The Puerto Rican National Guard was cofounded by Luis R. Esteves, the first Puerto Rican and Hispanic to graduate from West Point, where he tutored a young Dwight D. Eisenhower, the man who would become World War II's supreme commander of American forces and a US President.

Writing *Storm Dog* steeped me in the astounding devotion and love possible between dogs and their humans. Ariel's story also crystallized my absolute faith in the healing delight, the soulful discovery, and the ennobling power of music, nature, and our seemingly boundless imaginations.

Now . . . go out and express yourself. The world awaits to marvel at you and what you can think of and create. What will you do, as the poet Mary Oliver once wrote, "with your one wild and precious life?"